MATE ABDUCTION

AN ALIEN ABDUCTION STORY

EVE LANGLAIS

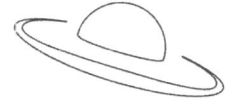

ONE

"YOU COW, GIVE THAT BACK," Katrina screeched from the common room the women all shared.

"If you want it, come and get it," goaded Anne. She'd been picking fights a lot lately. They all had.

Clarabelle sighed as she stared at her ceiling and the scraps of paper she'd stuck to it. Bits and pieces of posters and images of a world she could barely remember.

Earth. Her home, until the aliens abducted her and the girls she now called sisters. Seven of them in total. And all of them annoying twats.

She grimaced as Katrina bellowed, "I am going to make you eat dingus paste if you don't give it back!"

"Maybe if you asked nicely," sweet-spoken Sade tried to interject.

"You and your be-nice crap!" exclaimed Josee, who'd recently shaved her head and gotten her nose pierced. "Stop it already. Do you know this idiot said, 'Excuse me' when she took me down in the ring?"

"I didn't want to hurt you," Sade replied. She hadn't yet embraced the savage culture they'd been thrust into.

"You allowed yourself to be distracted, which is why I put you on your ass and then dumped you in the animal trough."

Which had been full of foul-smelling slop at the time. Sade had risen from it cursing. Considering she was usually the peacemaker, it proved impressive.

Everyone's temper ran short these days, but then again, what could you expect when an active group of young women in their twenties—or so Clarabelle assumed given time passed differently in space—were cooped together in a strange place with alien customs. Literally.

Say hello to planet Zonia... At least that was the name Clarabelle had given it. She'd heard fancier titles and complicated pronunciations that involved some clicking and, in one case, spit. She stuck to the humanized version in a place that was so strange and never did feel like home.

Years ago, Clarabelle and the other teenage girls were kidnapped by pirate slavers while on a school trip. Thankfully, they were rescued, and at the time, she'd kind of expected to be sent back to Earth. Wrong!

Apparently returning abductees to their home worlds went against the rules—making all those humans claiming they'd been taken and probed liars. Forget going home. Instead, Clarabelle and the other girls taken from Earth ended up on Zonia—minus their teacher who, after a dual abduction by purple mercenaries, fell in love and chose to live with her two mates. The teenage girls suffered a culture shock from the moment they landed on the planet ruled by a matriarchal race known as the Zonians. Frightening bitches with a single breast, taloned feet, and rapier gazes. Like a cross between a harpy and Amazon, but meaner.

Females ruled in this place by might and wit and fists. Education came with bruises but was never done maliciously. It was just the cost of learning. Making mistakes could hurt, so the simple concept was do it right to avoid damage.

Tough love, but make no mistake, Clarabelle was thankful for everything the Zonians had done. They'd shown her how to be strong. To defend herself. She had a bed, a roof over her head—most of the time—and plenty of food to eat. She had friends. But all those things didn't curb the yearning for home.

Or at least a place where people wouldn't cluck their tongues when she insisted on a private room for doing her business. Somewhere with humans who didn't think a slap or a bruise was a sign of affection—punch-buggy smacks excepted of course.

Not that she was abused. Never that. But the Zonians, as a warrior race, lacked gentle manners.

The thumping and yelling in the other room continued, and Clarabelle finally rose from her bed to stretch. Her gaze fell on the poster of a man. His skin tone was that of a human, a very pale pink, and his teeth were white and flat edged. He didn't sport a sword or pistol but rather a smile.

Her fingers traced his features. The very concept of a man remained as ephemeral as a dream. She'd not seen a guy since their arrival. Not a human one at any rate.

"Ha. Suck it. I win," Anne crowed, triumphant in their scuffle.

The claim was followed by noisy tears.

That snapped Clarabelle out of her reverie, and she stepped from her room to see Anne hugging a sobbing Katrina while Sade wrung her hands.

The other girls were out doing their assigned chores or training. Day in and out, that was all they did. All they had to look forward to.

There had to be something more. Something better. Something more like home. But she wouldn't find it here.

With that thought in mind, she marched out of the habitat assigned to her and her adopted sisters, her step firm as she mentally prepared a speech. She didn't allow herself to be distracted as she weaved the hard-packed paths of dirt and crushed bone—because even in death, parts were recycled.

Out in space, resources were often scarce and the concept of preservation strong—mostly because the evolved races had learned their lessons a long time ago, unlike the humans supposedly. The stigma that came around dead bodies didn't exist. Meat was meat. Bone was a great building material. And if she didn't want her skull to turn into a bowl for soup, she needed to find a way off this world where she could have a normal life.

With chips.

She missed chips so badly.

Arriving at the heavily thatched home of her teacher slash roost mother, she knew better than to go inside. At this time of day, there was only one place Pantariste would be. The garden behind her habitat. Although the word garden was subjective. In some cultures, it meant a place of beautiful foliage, trimmed and bright. On Zonia, it was a graveyard where the sk'uul plants pushed up from the ground, seeded inside the buried entrails of both enemies slain in battle and friends alike.

Clarabelle caught sight of Pantariste's bent form as she patted the ground, tamping down the dirt over her newest planting. Her roost mother—a term used for the one overseeing a nest of hatchlings, in this case human ones—never turned her head as Clarabelle approached, but she did snap, "What do want?"

Forget her hastily prepared speech. Clarabelle blurted out, "I want a spaceship."

"Just a spaceship? Greedy child. Making such a lofty demand. Perhaps you'd like a moon to go with it?" was the sarcastic retort. "Mayhap a few stars?"

Clarabelle knew better than to cower and retract her words. "Now you're just being silly. I just need a ship capable of faster than light speed."

They had all kinds of fancy terms in space for how fast spaceships travelled. Warp, slide, jump, whatever. She just knew it got people from point A to B with sometimes an odd stop at an alternate universe C.

"Just a ship, caw?" Pantariste pretended to muse over the request, and Clarabelle held her breath. "Despite your annoying way of asking, it turns out I have a vessel docked in the cavern."

The cavern being their version of a spaceport, hidden from eyes in the sky. There were a few of them scattered around, linked by tunnels and traps for the unwary who thought they could come and dominate the planet and its inhabitants.

Not that anyone dared, a fact often lamented by the Zonians. Their reputation preceded them.

"Can I have the ship?" Clarabelle asked.

"I wouldn't have mentioned it if you couldn't."

She blinked. It seemed a bit too easy. "Aren't you going to ask me why I need it?"

Pantariste uttered a noise and waved a taloned hand. "I'd say it's obvious. You and the other human orphans aren't content."

True and yet Clarabelle hastened to say, "We are grateful for everything—"

Her roost mother cut her off. "You jabber about things I already know. Of course, you are grateful. But unhappy. Understandable given you've entered your fertile season. It's natural for you to seek others of your kind, males more specifically, to dominate."

"Um, find people yes, but I don't care if they're male or not." A tiny white lie. She wouldn't mind the rumble of a deep voice. She'd been sixteen when she was abducted, and not exactly innocent. Years of only girls for company had left her yearning for something more.

"You should care. How will you procreate and continue your line without proper males?"

With the Zonians, it was all about the family and ensuring their legacy lived on. For the human girls, though, that was an impossible dream, as Zonian males weren't exactly anatomically compatible.

Not to mention the competition to claim one could be fierce. A human, even a well-trained one, would struggle against a pure blood Zonian in the mating heat.

"Not all of us want to make babies," she grumbled.

The idea of a grubby mini person demanding her

attention did not appeal. However, in the same stroke, she knew some of her friends were hoping to one day have a family.

"But the making of them is so enjoyable." Pantariste's beak spread in a lascivious smile. "If it is just coital pleasure you seek, then we could arrange something with the Kulin. They're almost decent warriors. I could speak to Aylia about an exchange."

Aylia was another human. Older than Clarabelle and her sisters, she'd been living with the Zonians since she was much younger than they had been on arrival. She'd gone off planet to find a baby daddy and ended up shacking up with him on some planet with a pretty ocean. Even Louisa, the only adult kidnapped with them, had decided to put her future and love in the hands of a pair of bumbling purple idiots.

Two guys, one girl. A decadent alien thing. Clarabelle wasn't greedy, she'd be content with one fellow, but to find one she needed that ship, which meant saying no to Pantariste's offer to import some dick.

"Don't even mention the Kulin." Clarabelle's nose wrinkled. "I hate the color purple, and they're kind of controlling."

Then there was the fact their sharply filed teeth scared the piss out of her. What if in the throes of passion the purple dude ripped out her throat? She hated that her mind saw them as so different. But she couldn't help it. She'd not been raised to see aliens as potential boyfriends. She had a hard time imagining herself with someone so different.

"If they are insolent, then you beat it out of them." Pantariste rolled her eyes and clacked her beak.

"Or maybe, instead, I could find a colony with a bunch of guys. Maybe even human guys," she added quickly. Without the extra parts or, in the case of the Kulin, missing balls. Was it really asking for much to have a boyfriend with teeth not meant for puncturing or fingers that didn't end in claws? No tentacles or tails either, just a nice, normal, guy.

"I know of no such place." Quick and dismissive.

"You haven't even looked," Clarabelle exclaimed.

"It is not my task to complete."

"You're right; it's not your task but mine. There has to be somewhere I can find more of my kind." If she and her sisters ended up Zonia, who was to say other abductees hadn't clustered in another place?

"As far as I know, the only other humans are on your origin planet, and visiting that galaxy is forbidden." Because the Zonians were big on following the rules. Meaning no going home to Earth.

Hearing it again didn't make it easier than the first time. They'd been warned at a young age they could never return. The orphans had seen too much, learned about the wider universe and its many inhabitants. Earth, with its protected status and easily panicked populace, wasn't ready for the truth.

"I know the rules. I wasn't planning to go there." Not at first. She'd have to be sly about her return, or the galactic cops would go after her. "There has to be somewhere else with humans. We can't be the only ones out here."

Given the abductions over the centuries, and the way humanity had of multiplying, it seemed logical there'd be a location where they'd flourished. Even if there wasn't, she wanted to get off this planet. Wanted... something. She'd know it when she found it.

Apparently Pantariste's seeming acquiescence was but a sham, as she began to hammer Clarabelle. "And if there isn't a place? What if you cannot find others like yourself? Or let's say you do find a male, maybe even a few? What if there aren't enough for all of you? What then?"

"Then we keep looking for more. The universe is huge." She waved a hand.

"It is, and your kind are rare and fragile. The chance of success is slim."

"I know that, and yet I won't give up hope."

"Never said you should, but there is more than one kind of male compatible with your race." Pantariste once again reminded her that there were purple dudes and even blue ones that could do the trick.

But Clarabelle wasn't interested in dating a Smurf.

"Human or not, it doesn't matter. The fact is there is no one here on Zonia for us. We have to leave to find boyfriends."

"The universe can be harsh."

"So can I." Clarabelle lifted her chin. "Besides, isn't it you who taught me to fight for what I want?"

"Since when do you obey your lessons?"

A reminder that Clarabelle had been a hard student to teach, stubborn and not only because of her red hair. She'd railed against their strange new life even as she adapted quickly to it. A part of her enjoyed the sparring and the camaraderie that came with living amongst the Zonians.

But she also missed Earth with its colorful fashions

and French fries. She craved a burger and dance music loud enough to make her body vibrate. And of late, she missed the shy hand holding and hot kisses in the back of a car where the windows steamed.

"I have to do this. I can't stay here." Or she'd be the one picking fights with her orphan sisters and sobbing for no reason.

"Very well. You have my permission."

As Clarabelle opened her mouth to argue, her brain clued in. "Wait. You mean I can go?"

"Of course. I was merely questioning you to ensure the purity of your purpose. You will depart immediately. The ship you'll be taking is already fully stocked with supplies for your journey."

"How did you know to get it ready? What if I didn't pass your test?"

"I know you. And your sisters. It's time for you to fly the nest." Pantariste cackled. "Although it took you long enough to ask. Aylia was younger than you when she went questing."

Probably because Aylia was raised to think she needed to get preggers.

"Does it have auto pilot?" Because now that she'd gotten the ship, a problem arose. She didn't know how to drive one.

"Idiot." Pantariste snorted. "You'll take Ishtara with you."

Another of her teachers, but much younger than the rest, Ishtara sometimes hung out with Clarabelle. She liked to think they were friends. Having her along would help a lot.

"What do I do if I find a place that has everything we need?" Clarabelle asked.

"Send word that we might inform your sisters. They shall have the choice to join you."

Clarabelle wanted to do cartwheels. Instead she wrapped her arms around Pantariste and exclaimed, "Thank you."

"Don't thank me yet. This quest of yours might end in failure, which is why you will not tell anyone about it."

"Not even my sisters?"

"Could they handle the disappointment?"

Clarabelle realized that she couldn't raise their hopes and then possibly dash them. "I won't say a word."

Pantariste waved. "Off with you before I change my mind."

She ran before that could happen. It took her only a few minutes to pack but longer to say goodbye to her sisters. She hugged them and when asked where she was going would only say that she was going on a voyage with Ishtara to space. Which, needless to say, caused some jealousy.

It was especially hard for her to lie to her best friend, Betty.

"There's something you're not telling me," Betty accused.

Clarabelle clasped her sister's hands. "I'll send you messages."

"Promise?"

"Promise," she said, hugging her best friend.

Then it was on to sweet and shy Sade, who looked lost as she hugged herself, her blonde hair spilling over her shoulders. A fragile soul, she'd not adapted well to the violence and fighting on Zonia.

"Don't let them walk all over you," Clarabelle reminded softly.

Sade sighed. "I wish I could be more like you. Fearless. Adventuring."

"One day you'll have a grand adventure of your own," Clarabelle declared.

Sade snorted. "Ha. Next thing you'll be saying I'll find a husband."

"You never know. Louisa found two."

"Bring back a couple," was Katrina's demand. "We can share."

Which spawned some good-natured arguing, with Josee declaring she didn't need a man to satisfy her.

Clarabelle skipped out the door before they could see her tears. It was harder than expected to leave them, especially without telling the truth. Did they suspect her story was a lie?

It didn't matter. She owed them. She couldn't fail.

The cavern where the ships were kept retained its rocky ceiling, though it was sprayed with a clear coat of something that made it crack-proof. It could withstand a direct blast from most weapons capable of firing in space. She'd declined a live demonstration.

It was freaking huge and could hold up to fifty ships. It was buzzing with activity, most of the scurrying bodies small and orange, their four arms and a tail making them quick with tools. They swarmed over the ships, fixing things and jabbering in a strange language.

The Zonians among them appeared gigantic, and yet

everyone got along. The business arrangement with the Psalandrs saw both sides winning.

Only one ship wasn't crawling with mechanics. She aimed for it. The gangplank extended from the bottom, and her boots clanked on it as she boarded the ship.

And paused, feeling a little dizzy. She braced herself and swallowed hard. This was it. She was really doing this, leaving her home, her family.

Oh shit.

Deep breath.

Fear was but an emotion, and she could control it. She reminded herself that people flew on these ships all the time.

Some didn't return.

Most did, with wondrous stories.

Her turn to leave and discover what was out there.

Her nerves steadied, and she stepped past the embarkation chamber. A fancy term for the tiny room that could seal shut and spit you into space. She remembered the movies on Earth.

The hall proved smooth walled, like the ceiling, which extended to about ten feet. It was tall enough and wide enough for a Zonian. She traced her fingers over the paneling with its almost imperceptible seams. Fine work. The Psalandrs, of course. The Zonians had no patience or time to build ships, but they had the wealth to buy them. Protection, food, and other things were given to the orange mechanics, and in return, they built and maintained the technology.

"Stop petting the walls and get in here," Ishtara's voice barked from a speaker.

To the casual observer, she might sound angry. All the

Zonians spoke in that same manner. In the beginning, Clarabelle had mistaken it for them being mean. She knew now that Pantariste and the others would lay down their lives for her and anyone they considered family.

Entering the bridge, she found Ishtara sitting in the command seat.

A yellow gaze fixed on her, and the beak smirked. "There you are. Taking your lazy time. Don't look so impatient to me. Perhaps you don't really want to go on this trip, caw?"

"Just because I didn't run all the way here doesn't mean I'm not pumped about this mission."

"Mission!" Ishtara snorted. "I believe Katrina would call it a booty call, given we are hunting for breeding stock."

"That's a rather nasty way of putting it."

Her indignation had Ishtara grinning. "Would you prefer I call your males dinner?"

"Not funny, Ish," she grumbled as she tossed her pack on the floor and sat in her seat. She'd stow it later.

"You know, if it's human males you need, then we could pop into the Obsidian market and see what we can bid on."

"*We*," Clarabelle enunciated, "don't want slaves. We want boyfriends." The word didn't really translate despite the emitter embedded inside her ear.

"Why would you be friends with a male?" The very idea flummoxed Ishtara.

"Because they're fun to talk to. They make you feel special when they flirt. Sometimes it's nice to just cuddle."

"If you wish for hugs, I will give you one that you

won't forget." Ishtara cracked her knuckles, and Clarabelle waved her off before she could break some bones.

"I don't want a hug from you. Or my sisters."

"Only from a male? Why?"

"Because it's different. Nice. When you cuddle with someone you care about, it's special and makes you feel warm inside." She struggled to explain something she barely understood herself. It had been a while since her time on Earth. "I want to find a companion. A human one that will understand me. Not a slave or someone whose sperm I'm going to take before I ditch him. I—I mean *we*," she hastily corrected, "want a real chance for a connection on an emotional level. Maybe if we meet the right guy we'll have a kid with them, although I'm not going to be the one staying home. If I end up with a baby daddy, he could take care of the runt."

"You'd share the raising of progeny with a male?" Ishtara sounded aghast. "You'll ruin them. What if the male's weakness is passed on?"

"But that's just it. On Earth, men and women are basically equal." For the most part. There were some inequalities still, but nothing like the drastic difference she'd experienced since going to space. Space-travelling aliens were not as progressive as expected.

"On Earth, mayhap this impossibility occurs, but you are here, on Zonia."

"Yeah, but we're not Zonian." She probably shouldn't have shouted it.

"Obviously." The yellow gaze flicked up and down. "Very well, you have convinced me. Let us go find you some pale-skinned, penile-possessing companions."

Clarabelle wanted to bang her head off the console at

the less-than-eloquent description. But she had no time for annoyance, as they soon left the planet side bay and were airborne. She didn't have a window to look out, but she did have a screen, and she watched avidly as they left the surface of the planet, a ball of browns and yellows with some toxic green for water. An alien world with a few too many suns. They left it behind to coast among the stars.

Holy crap, she'd done it. She was on a quest to find the orphans a new home. Despite Pantariste's, and even Ishtara's, less-than-enthusiastic responses, she hoped to soon be able to provide her sisters with coordinates for a planet where they would thrive.

Her optimism didn't last.

TWO

HIS HOPE FADED.

Thyos stood at the base of the clan tree, the symbol of their strength. Its branches spread wide, the bark white. The last of its leaves clung valiantly. A pang struck as he stared up the dying monument that refused to flourish despite all his efforts. It had been several seasons since it produced seeds. Not since his father died. As if the tree of life mourned his passing.

Or so Thyos liked to believe. According to his mother, the falling leaves and the lack of seeds were all his fault because he'd not yet mated.

In order for a clan tree to thrive, its leader needed to be wedded and at least attempting to breed the next generation. Practicing with his hand didn't count.

It should be noted Thyos was more than willing to bind himself to someone. He just couldn't seem to find himself a mate. Not for lack of trying.

As he pursued the available options, which weren't as many as previous generations, a sickness having taken many females of mating age, he found himself discouraged. Could it be he'd failed to recognize the bond that indicated he'd found his *sykyrah*? His fated one.

Everyone had a perfect match. Most could take their time to find it. Thyos didn't have that luxury if he wanted to remain clan leader.

He placed his hand on the bark, the flesh moist and pulsing. He closed his eyes and hoped for a sign. A gentle breeze to give him direction. Even the projection of a word or the name of the one he sought.

Surely his mate existed somewhere on this planet. Or had she died before they found the cure to the illness that took only the females? Was he to be the last leader of his clan? Destined to die childless and alone among the ruins of a once great legacy?

Never.

He pushed away from the tree and glared at it. "I'm doing my best."

And failing. Meaning he failed all who relied on him. A leader without his *sykyrah* translated into a clan with no future. No one understood why the bond was needed, only that without it the paired couples within that tribe couldn't procreate. All because the tree refused to seed.

"Would you at least give me a direction? A name would be nice," he drawled sarcastically.

"You do realize the tree can't speak." The amused statement had him transferring his scowl to Karymma, the clan's shaman and the voice for the goddess Karma.

Karymma stopped before him, her long gray robes almost touching the ground, the sleeves hiding her hands, the cowl casting her features in shadow.

"I don't know what else it expects me to do." He

waved a hand at the life tree. "I've searched this entire planet looking for my mate. She doesn't exist." Or she'd perished before he found her. If that were the case, then they were doomed. Best he begin the process of parceling off his tribespeople before the tree withered and died.

"Fear not, Thyos the Brave, she exists." The voice of the shaman changed, and suddenly he no longer spoke with Karymma. The goddess visited through her mortal conduit. That didn't make his irritation any less.

"Where?" he growled. "I've paid a visit to every clan on the planet. More than once." Had the scars to prove it, given a few of them weren't on pleasant terms with his tribe.

"Your chosen is not of any clan," the goddess stated.

That was rather specific. His brows lifted. "If she's not with any of the clans, then where? Why is she hiding?" And did this mean his goddess thought to pair him with a coward? Because only a weakling would attempt to circumvent fate.

"She isn't hiding. She is simply not here." Karymma pointed to the sky. "Your bride is up there."

He glanced upward and couldn't help but frown as he saw the vast wingspan of the flesh-rending tarodact, the four limbs beating as it soared on a hot wind. "I'm not mating with a bird."

"Don't be foolish. I mean your mate isn't on this planet."

The rebuke brought an even deeper frown. "Then which planet?" Because, in this solar system alone, another eight were inhabited, and only two of them had peace treaties with his at the moment.

"Do you really expect me to just give you the answer?"

As he glanced at Karymma, he blinked. For a moment he perceived two people, one being the old woman from his village, the other young and fresh faced, beautiful and dangerous. His goddess. Another blink and she was gone.

"Given I am running out of time, a plain answer would be helpful, yes." Because he never did do well at solving riddles.

"How about a hint? She's not from your star system. As a matter of fact, she comes from far, far away."

The implication was not lost on him. "You expect me to marry a non-blood?" His lip curled. "As if I'd taint the family line."

"You do not have a choice."

His stubborn side rose. He didn't care if the goddess spoke. "I refuse to believe that. You must be mistaken." His rebuke amounted to blasphemy. No one gainsaid the goddess. Even if she chose to speak through the shaman. It was expected he would listen. Obey.

"Insolence." The word emerged on a soft exhalation, and yet it lashed him with icy pellets.

His breath frosted, as did Karymma's skin. From the frozen statue stepped his goddess, in the flesh, the heat of her radiating and yet not dispelling the chill in his veins.

Even he wasn't so dumb as to remain standing. He hit the ground on one knee. "My goddess does me honor."

She snorted, and the icy sensation vanished. "You are utterly insolent yet endearing anyhow. Rise, my warrior."

Thyos stood and tucked his hands behind his back. "I apologize for my rudeness, Goddess."

"Apology accepted. Mostly because you will have a difficult task." Karma perused him. "A good thing you're pretty, or this might not work. Your mate will be more stubborn than you."

"You know of her?"

"Enough to discern the difficulties. You are very different."

"She's an alien, then?" he asked, hoping he'd misunderstood.

"If you go back enough generations, you come from the same seed but have changed along the way. Which is a good thing because we must look beyond our world to others if we are to bring strength and vitality back to this world." She trailed her fingers on the bark of the tree, and where she touched, the white-gray bark turned a dark brown. A few leaves budded.

She gave it a hint of life. Gave him a little more time.

He appreciated it, but still, an alien as his mate? "My mother will not be pleased." She tended to be a strong proponent of pure bloodlines.

"Your mother will obey. As will you."

Thyos struggled to agree. To hand over the fate of his future to a goddess who could be capricious. History clearly showed that sometimes her intervention led to sorrow—for the losers in the wars she started. The winners all adored her while the losers tried to regain her favor.

"Is there not someone else?"

"Enough arguing. You can keep wandering, looking uselessly on this world, or you can face the truth and the future."

"Let's say I believe you. How am I supposed to find my mate?" Far, far away sounded like the start to a fantasy story.

"The hand of fate will guide you."

"It better guide me accurately. There are millions of planets and stars. Where would I even start my search?

"That's just it. You don't need to search. Part of the magic of the mating bond is the guarantee you'll find her." Karma beamed as if that were the best answer ever.

Not even close. He couldn't help a sarcastic, "Will this magic also give me a ship and a reason to leave?" Because their hangar currently sat empty. Their few ships already out on missions.

"Have faith."

In the blink of one eye and the next, the goddess was gone and Karymma swayed in place, a beatific smile on her face that turned to a sharp rebuke when he didn't move fast enough for her liking.

"You heard our goddess. Go find your intended."

"How about she finds me?" he grumbled as he headed back to his home, a village in the province of Qhryce.

As he trod the familiar path, he thought over what his goddess said. Could he truly find his mate and save not only his future but that of his tribe?

Hard to believe given, as he entered the village, he couldn't help but notice the signs of even more abandonment. The longer he went without fulfilling his duties, the more his people absconded in the night. He couldn't blame the couples who didn't want to wait any longer to breed.

It shamed him that the once powerful tribe he'd inherited had weakened all because he failed. Failed to find his *sykyrah*.

And now Karma claimed his mate wasn't even here.

That he'd have to leave to find her. Hard to accomplish without a vessel.

"Thyos, about time you showed up." Kryx, his friend and acting second-in-command, strode out of the door to Thyos's ever-evolving habitat.

Thyos's grandfather had begun the process, sculpting a patch of *lahpee*—a living rock that literally grew and could be coaxed into forms. It resulted in homes sculpted to their needs. By the truly adept, it became pieces of structural art. Currently the formation boasted three stories with sloped windows, sturdy balconies, and a fireplace that rose through the middle and heated the entire home.

He'd looked forward to adding another floor when he found his mate and expanded his family. Instead, this place would crumble into ruin when the bond died out with him.

He tried to not dwell on it. "What are you doing here? I thought you were on a scouting trip." Anything to avoid a matchmaking mother, which used to be his mother's enjoyment, too. Now she sighed loudly and often about how she'd never have any grandchildren to spoil.

She wasn't subtle in her efforts.

"My trip got cut short. I was called back by the emperor."

The emperor was the one being capable of ruling all the tribes. As emperors went, theirs tended to not get involved too often in clan affairs. Unless it would harm the planet as a whole.

"What did he want?"

"To assign me a new quest," Kryx replied with nonchalance.

"Lucky," Thyos muttered.

"I'm glad you said that." Kryx beamed. "Because you're coming with me."

Immediately, Thyos's expression brightened. "Are we going on a hunt?" He wouldn't mind something to take the edge off his frustration.

"Of sorts."

"Protection detail?" It wouldn't be the first time the emperor assigned them a diplomatic task.

"There will be no fighting if all goes well. Which is a good thing given we're going off planet."

Away from Qhryce? He wouldn't usually be bothered, but given the dire state of his tree, if he left, would he have anything left to come back to? "Exactly what does this mission entail?"

"We need to retrieve something."

"Since when does trading require the emperor getting involved?" Not to mention, why drag him along? A leader's place wasn't as a bargaining merchant acquiring supplies but with his clan, keeping it safe.

"Because this is a very special item." Kryx grinned widely, and it didn't assuage Thyos's concerns one bit.

"Why me? Why not Jyni or Lynna?"

"Because the emperor asked for you."

His confusion coiled even tighter. "You know this isn't a good time for me."

"All the more reason we have to leave promptly. Karma stressed that point very strongly when she had her audience with the emperor."

He blinked. "Karma spoke to Nyro?" He couldn't help the suspicious note in the query.

"At length, or so I heard. I wasn't privy to the details,

only the result that you are to find your *sykyrah* and, according to our goddess, you have to leave Qhryce to do so."

Thyos sent her up silent prayer—*Nice meddling.* She'd known he'd balk and find excuses to not leave, so she'd forced his hand.

"Did the goddess give you a coordinate?"

Kryx shook his head. "Not exactly. What I do have is a list of trading posts we're supposed to visit."

"Wander aimlessly in the hopes we accidentally find my mate?" He arched a brow. "Am I the only one that finds that a tad farfetched?"

Kryx's grin turned lopsided as he shrugged. "Sounds crazy, I know, but it can't hurt to try. We've tried everything else."

A reminder that Kryx had crossed the planet with him in search of his *sykyrah*. He had to wonder if his friend had yet realized he'd run into the same problem of not finding his mate.

"It's impossible."

"Are you already admitting defeat?" Kryx taunted.

"Never."

Which was how he ended up with his friend on a sleek cruiser flying from station to station, ignoring the harangues from his mother back home, all too aware of the ticking of time. Each destination they left without finding his mate only served to deepen his despair. It didn't help that the last transmission from his mother had informed him that more of his people had fled. They'd lost faith in him.

If he didn't do something, and soon, he'd have no clan to return to.

"Prepare for docking."

The computerized announcement had him dressing and arming himself for excursion. Given the stations often held a deep chill, he chose a thick cloak, long and voluminous. It concealed his identity and many weapons. Only idiots went around unarmed.

The station, Lost Hope, was tethered to a moon, meaning it sprawled all over the place with transportation tubes connecting the various hubs. After sending over the correct number of credits—a large amount not worth the dirty locale—they were given a docking berth where they could disembark. As he travelled the interconnecting tubes, aimlessly for the most part, he took note of the many species roaming around. Mostly male with a few females either being tightly accompanied for safety or openly wielding more weapons than even he carried.

None made his heart pound. None grabbed his attention. Doubtful he'd find his *sykyrah* here, and he was beginning to reach the point he didn't care anymore.

He missed home. Wanted to be with his tree when it exhaled its last. To be there to apologize to it and any who were affected by his failure.

Then, when it was over, and his failure was complete, he planned to get extremely drunk and remain that way until he died in battle—which could be quickly depending on his level of sobriety. It had worked for his great-uncle Phanos.

It's time I admitted defeat. He'd tell Kryx his decision once they'd concluded their business here.

He already knew his friend would argue because Thyos had asked after the last two stops if they were going home yet. Each time, Kryx replied, "Not until we find her."

And by her he could have meant the *sykyrah* for either of them, because Thyos wasn't the only one looking for his mate. He'd seen Kryx eyeing the females with more than passing interest.

As he pivoted on the moving walkway that brought travelers through the various tube systems, Thyos felt an odd tug. Before he could ponder the sensation, he'd stepped onto solid ground.

He found himself in the marketplace dome anchored to the moon with solid rock underfoot, swept clean of dust. Buildings crowded the area, many with flashing signs advertising their wares—a glass for a tavern, breasts for sex, and a blood splatter for food.

It was the alley between a restaurant boasting the best-tasting rat skewers in town and a massage parlor featuring a nine-armed attendant that drew his attention.

Cloak swirling around his ankles, he approached but didn't enter the slim passageway. He could clearly see a female of pale complexion, the flesh of her cheeks and nose covered in light spots. A flash of orange turned out to be hair pulled back from her face but loose down her back in a wild riot of curls.

The female needed a tan. Perhaps a good scrubbing. Definitely some more meat on her bones. Not that he cared what she ate.

Thyos couldn't even say why he kept eyeing her. She wasn't of a species he'd encountered before, despite being similar to his own with a pair of arms and legs, recognizable facial features, and two breasts like the females of his world.

And nothing else. Not even a pair of sexy horns or stubby sensitive wings. In his youth, he lamented the fact he wasn't blessed with any, but he made up for it in strength.

As he turned to move away, he noticed a gang approaching, several large males in varying states of rankness, from putrid to possibly dead and not knowing it yet. A quick glance showed them entering the alley where the alien female stood.

He should walk away. None of his business. Instead, he positioned himself to spy on what happened.

The gang confronted the woman, their body language and jeers ripe with promises of violence.

Still not his problem. She was a stranger. A no-one not worth the effort. He couldn't have even said why he gave her a second glance.

And a third.

There was no denying she intrigued him. His sluggish blood began to pump in his veins. His attention narrowed in on her and the surrounding danger.

If he didn't act, she would probably get hurt. Maybe even die.

She needed a hero.

She needs me.

THREE

"SUBMIT, FEMALE," the fellow with tusks jutting through his chin grunted.

Here we go again. It was a mistake, agreeing to meet Buurg away from the bar. However, when the tusked alien sidled close, his smell arriving before his whispered, "I have info," she'd been relieved to finally encounter someone with something to offer.

But he refused to divulge anything in the bar, claiming the information was too secret and valuable to discuss in public. And her stupid, desperate ass believed him. Because hey, who didn't meet in a dark alley to exchange information?

Buurg didn't come alone, and she didn't need to see the leers of his companions to realize they weren't up to any good.

Clarabelle wanted to sigh but instead settled for muttering, "Why, oh why, is it that the universe over, when males are presented with a female, you get so monumentally stupid?"

Since leaving Zonia, she'd encountered nothing but disappointment. Planet after planet, space stations and outposts alike, all presented her with males of all types. Some almost appeared human until they blew fire from their noses or their fingertips suctioned to skin and the sweat right from the glands. Severing them broke the seal, and she didn't feel like apologizing one bit when Vampire Fingers complained. Served him right for not asking first.

So many different types of men but, in many respects, they were the same when it came to their attitudes toward women. You would think the universe would be a more evolved place...

You would be wrong.

While the Zonians commanded respect, little human girls didn't. Meaning they had to leave more than one place quickly, as Clarabelle showed little patience for unwanted overtures. For the moment, Ishtara found it amusing to keep track of the bodies they left behind; however, Clarabelle knew her friend's patience frayed the longer their quest took without finding any promising leads.

Once Clarabelle finished her business in the alley, they'd be crossing the Lost Hope space station off their list too.

She tapped the comm unit on her chest and muttered, "Prep for departure."

"Already?" Ishtara cawed in her earpiece.

"Who you talking to?" barked Buurg, obviously the leader of the gang of thugs.

"Do you mind?" Clarabelle snapped. "I'm conversing with my friend."

"Friend. Ha!" was Ishtara's exclamation in her earpiece. "Deal with your company and get your scrawny buttocks back to the ship." Ishtara didn't insult Clarabelle by asking if she needed help.

"I should just be a few minutes." She still referred to time in Earth terms, unable—and unwilling—to change her language to the universal standards, which involved clicks and revolutions and weird terms that meant nothing to her.

"There is no escape." Burg did his best to sound ominous. Little did he know she'd faced worse.

"You really might want to rethink this," she said.

"Submit!"

She flexed her fingers as the thugs circled her, thinking they had her trapped. She might not have spent her time since birth learning to fight like the renowned Zonian Aliya, but she wasn't a slouch when it came to protecting herself. While she had shit aim when it came to firearms, she was rather handy with knives.

Before the thug with two fingers and smacking bulbous lips could grab hold, she'd slashed across the top of his hand, drawing a startled hiss then an exclamation as severed fingers hit the floor. Her primary blade, with its deceptively sleek appearance, was sharp enough to slice through anything—metal or flesh, even bone, all parted like butter.

Before blood could spurt, she whirled and tossed her other dagger right into the shoulder of the next closest assailant. It punched right through, and only a loss of momentum kept it from piercing the wall behind and disappearing into another room.

The third wanna-be suitor—who had only four teeth

left in his mouth and breath that watered the eyes—managed to grab hold of the back of her neck. He squeezed as he cackled. "Enough of dat, miss—Oof."

He grunted as she rammed her elbow into his gut, and as he sucked in a wheezing breath, she slammed her heel into his thigh. The blow itself wasn't why he dropped to the floor but rather the hidden blade that shot from her heel, activated by the intentional wiggle of her large toe. The blade had a sleeping agent as well just in case a slice wasn't enough. He went down and stayed down.

Judging by the garbled yelling, she still had two more to go. The idiots didn't learn by example but stuck around.

She ducked just as a meaty fist swung overhead. The training to move quickly came in useful, or she'd have been knocked into the next galaxy. Before the fist could rewind for a second shot, she popped up and pulled two more blades from her thigh sheaths.

Jab. Thrust. She drove them into two of the three thighs. When Buurg yelled, "You stabbed my dick!" she realized she'd missed one of the legs, making her briefly wonder—*How the hell did he figure it would fit?*

It was a good thing he wouldn't get a chance to try. She pulled her blades loose, the edges wet with brilliant blue blood. She made no sound of warning as she pivoted and lightly tossed them at the last target. They landed with meaty thuds, embedded to the hilt.

The corpulent alien glanced down at them, and one of his eyestalks developed a twitch. A tentacle grabbed the knife and pulled it free as a dark green ichor leaked.

But the alien dude didn't fall down. Rather he

grinned from a spot around his middle, his entire torso splitting open into a huge mouth. The smile didn't reassure.

Someone rushed her, slamming their shoulder into her body, the impact lifting her off the ground and thudding her into a wall.

For a moment, all breath escaped and she saw stars and a long bright tunnel. Her feet dangled off the ground, and Clarabelle wondered if this was how she would die.

Like Hell. She was too young to give up.

Rage had her sucking in a breath. She coiled herself in preparation and kicked the alien with the fetid breath in the balls. Giant balls, she noticed, big and heavy enough they hung in the crotch of his pants.

As he gasped and loosened his grip, she twisted, hit the ground, and in the same motion pulled another knife and jabbed it into a swinging pendulum. She preferred to not think of what was in the white juice that jetted. The more important point being her assailant hit the ground in time for her to flip and see the mouth-belly alien opening wide.

She snarled, "Are you really that stupid?"

He was.

By the time she was done and stood over him, knives dripping, he had a few more mouths in the form of slashing wounds.

Clap. Clap.

Seriously? Was she not done yet?

She looked up to see a rather large cloaked figure standing just outside of the spray of blood, gloved hands slapping together. In appreciation or challenge? She couldn't tell their intentions, nor even what race they were given their features were hidden by a hood.

"Move along," she snapped. "Nothing to see." Meanwhile, she took note of her used daggers. If she tossed the pair in her hands, she'd need to rearm herself, as she'd run out of blades unless she could use the one in her heel again.

"You fight well." The deep voice held a hint of accent despite the auditory translator she used. Male? He certainly had a deep timbre, but that meant nothing in the galaxies.

"If you add 'for a girl,' you'll learn just how well," was her grumbled reply.

"Why would I insult you?" He sounded surprised by the very idea.

"Because that's what everyone likes to do when they see a human." The other favorite thing involved trying to acquire her. Apparently, humans had some value as slaves.

"Human?" He repeated the word as if it were strange. "I am not familiar with your kind. From what system do you hail?"

"The Earth one."

"Never heard of it."

"Probably on account we're supposed to be protected and alien dudes aren't allowed to touch it."

"Yet here you are."

"You know what they say about the forbidden fruit," she muttered, moving sideways while watching him. She retrieved a blade and sheathed it.

For the moment, he appeared content to talk.

"Actually, I don't know. None of our fruit has been banned."

She blinked. She still forgot how the common expressions she took for granted often didn't translate. "It means telling someone they can't have something only makes it more tempting."

"On my planet we like to say, covet at your own peril."

"Which is more the Earth equivalent of 'touch it and die.'"

"Do you have many such edicts?"

She didn't understand his interest. "What do you want?"

"What makes you think I am in need of anything?"

"Because you're talking to me," was her blunt reply.

"You're intriguing."

"And not interested in becoming your property. If you try and take me, I will eviscerate you."

The low chuckle raised the hairs on her body. "I would never force you to do anything. But Karma might."

"Who is Karma?"

"Not a goddess to mess with," he muttered.

Her snort held some disdain. "You aliens and your religion. I thought it was bad on Earth, but even out here, you believe in the impossible."

"Your Earth has no gods?" His query held genuine curiosity.

"Depends who you ask. Some think there is only one god, and they like to fight the ones who claim there are many." The blade she withdrew from quivering flesh showed the edges corroded by the acidic blood. Dammit. She cast a quick glare at the body at her feet. When it dared to move, she kicked it.

"We only have one goddess meddling in our affairs, which is quite enough." He spoke as if she were real.

"Good for you. Happy worshiping and all that. If you don't mind, I have somewhere else to be." The incident with the bullies hadn't yet drawn untoward attention, but she shouldn't tempt bad luck.

"Where do you travel?" he asked.

"As if I'm going to tell you," Clarabelle uttered on a snort as she collected the last of her blades and strode in the direction of the ship's dock.

"Your caution is admirable, but unnecessary." He kept pace with her, his cloak billowing and yet never revealing any limbs.

How many arms and legs did he hide under there?

"Where are *you* going?" she countered.

"Now that I've completed my task? Back to my home world."

"What kind of task?" she asked before she could stop herself.

"I was sent to find my mate."

The answer startled enough that she stumbled. "You went hunting for a wife? How'd it go?"

"Different than expected," he replied.

"Congratulations?" she ventured. She cast a glance at the large figure, curious now as to what hid under the fabric.

"Are you mated?" he asked.

"Nope."

"Pity," he muttered. "That might have offered reprieve."

"Meaning what?" She whirled and glared at him. "Are

you implying I shouldn't have a husband? That I'm not good enough?"

He eyed her up and down. "I'm sure you are more than fine, for some people."

The insult made her cheeks burn. "I pity the woman who is getting stuck with you."

"You should pity me. She's not what I wanted at all," he grumbled.

"Then why marry her?"

"Because if I don't, bad things will happen."

How ominous, and not her problem. "Well, good luck with whatever you have going on." She waved a hand in farewell and turned into a side corridor.

The big dude remained by her side.

"Those brigands that you dispatched, why were they after you?" he asked.

"Because I'm human. Duh. They wanted to rape me and then sell me."

"You conversed with them, though, before killing them."

"I did," she admitted, realizing only now just how long he'd been watching. And yet he'd never come to her aid...

"What did you ask them?"

Since he seemed intent, she quickly explained. "They were replying to some inquiries I'd made."

"Inquiries about what?"

She heaved a long sigh. "What is it with you and the questions?"

"I am a curious male."

She eyed him. Given his size, he was obviously of a large race, appearing two legged and armed, but that voluminous cloak could hide anything. She'd learned that lesson with Mr. Handsy-tail. If he didn't want to lose the tip, he should have kept its nosy probing to itself.

"Since you absolutely must know, I'm looking for humans. Others like me," she finally replied.

"Have you found many?"

"No. Or have you already forgotten that Earth is on a no-invasion list?"

"Meaning your species are not allowed out of their solar system," he muttered aloud. "Why not just return to your world?"

"Because, apparently, I know too much."

"Do you know where to find more of your kind?"

"Would I be meeting sketchy aliens in alleys if I did?"

He wasn't done with his interrogation. "What do you hope to find in a settlement of humans?"

Saying "a boyfriend" made her sound pathetic. "I don't see as that's any of your business."

"What if I have the information you seek?"

She snorted. "As of five minutes ago, you didn't even know humans existed."

"But I am knowledgeable. Perhaps I could help you."

"For what price?" She planted her hands on her hips. "Because we both know nothing comes for free."

"Kindness needs no payment."

"Kindness? Ha!" she couldn't help but exclaim. "I am not stupid, dude. You want something."

"You are correct. I require your help."

Given what she knew so far, it wasn't hard to surmise his need. "You want me to help you break your engagement, don't you? Because you don't like your fiancée."

"Not exactly. More like convince the female in question that the union is necessary."

She burst into laughter. "Dude, I am not going to con some lady into marrying you."

"But you'd be willing to help prevent the union?" he questioned as if to clarify.

"Damned straight, I would. I don't believe in forced or arranged marriage." She was an Earth girl, through and through, who wanted a relationship that would also be a partnership, equals, unless there was a spider to kill.

She used to think eight legs back home was bad. Add paralytic alien hair, a mouth big enough to take a fleshy bite, and a voice that could chirp like a chipmunk, "Don't move, I'm trying to eat." It was enough to send anyone into hiding.

"Help me with my bride situation and I'll help you."

"How?"

"I have connections. If a human colony exists, I will find it."

He sounded certain, but that didn't mean shit. "Give me verifiable info and I'll get your girlfriend to dump you."

"She is not my friend. And I wish to remain alive and not have my corpse dumped anywhere."

"Dude, it's slang. Don't take it so literally."

"Is 'dude' a term of affection?"

She beamed as she said, quite sincerely, "Why yes, yes, it is. And this…" She held up a middle finger. "And this means nice to make your acquaintance."

His reply? He held up his own finger and said, quite seriously, "Nice to meet you, too, *dood.*"

She almost hit the floor laughing.

FOUR

HER LIPS QUIRKED as if amused, making it obvious she lied about the word and gesture. Lied prettily, but then again, so had he.

He didn't need her to come between him and his mate because, against all odds, he'd found her. Looked right at her, a human with spotted skin and strange-colored hair, lacking any extra limbs or body parts. A warrior female who would probably spill his innards if he told her she was to be his bride.

Karma surely played a jest. This female couldn't be the one. Sure, she had a valiant heart and spirit, yet by her very words, she named herself barbarian. From a prohibited planet. Would she even be compatible with him?

He eyed her up and down. On that respect, he had no doubts they'd be well suited. The question being, would he survive the coitus? Knowing how well she wielded a knife, he could only wonder if she believed in the castration of males after she'd used them. More than a few races had such painful rituals, and it behooved a male fond of his genitalia to avoid them.

"Why are you staring at me like I'm going to turn into a monster?" she asked.

"What are your thoughts on castration?"

"Females, never. Males..." She eyed his groin area. "Depends on what they try to do with it." Her gaze slewed back to his face. "Why do you ask?"

He wasn't about to explain. "Are males of your kind rare?" He knew of a few species where the feminine genes outnumbered the masculine. The Lunurfs, for example— blue-skinned scientists with a strange honor code—had a shortage of males and were said to be resorting to the slave markets to find suitable seed.

On his own world, they also had issues which had been somewhat resolved with some females bonding with more than a few males at once. He'd wondered as he traveled to the different tribes in search of his mate if he'd end up part of a harem. However rather than share, according to Karma, he was expected to mate outside his kind with a female who showed no fear or common sense as she strutted into the busy docking area. He couldn't help but scan the environs and note the blatant interest in the human.

She drew all eyes, noses, and more than a few tentacles began slinking in her direction. Perhaps she exuded a pheromone that drew attention? Decontamination might eliminate the madness that consumed him. The jealousy that struck when they passed a group of mechanics and one of them dared to lift its tail, its eyeball staring in a way he didn't like.

Lightning quick, Thyos grabbed the appendage. "Disrespectful," he grumbled as he knotted the alien's offending arm tight. When done, he glared at the others who stared in open-jawed astonishment. "Anyone else care to stare?"

The rapid whirling of bodies led to her laughter. A husky sound that vibrated through him.

"Touchy, aren't you?"

"If you let them think you weak, they will strike. It's best to make a point early. It saves the bother of a full-scale vendetta later on."

She blinked at him. "A vendetta for staring?"

"Staring might lead to overtures and, when rebuffed, perhaps even an unfortunate attempt at abduction or assault."

"Why is that unfortunate?"

"Because minor infractions we can punish lightly." He gestured behind them to the alien screeching as his friends brought out a light saw. The limb he'd tied wouldn't be salvageable. "While the more severe are annihilated to provide a stern example."

"You don't come from a dense population, do you?"

"Our world is not overcrowded, if that is your query. Planetary sustainability requires us keeping the number of inhabitants at a certain level."

"Which I'm guessing in plain English means you have lots of wars so you don't multiply like rabbits and overrun the world."

"Not just wars. Vendettas, skirmishes, and if that isn't enough, we also have the games."

"The games being?"

"A sporting event, usually to the death, to prove valiance."

"Have you ever played?"

He grinned. "Yes." He'd won four of the tournaments, which was a matter of pride with his mother. It still didn't net him a bride.

Until now.

Did this human feel the connection? She gave no indication she did as she stomped for an open section in the bay where a ship sat docked, the gangway open.

"Yo, bitch tit, I'm back! And I have company," the orange-haired female yodeled.

He could only assume she spoke some odd dialect, as his translator had no comparison.

As if her words were a signal, the so-called bitch tit came thumping into view. Upon seeing the Zonian—distinctive with her avian legs ending in claws, the rapier features and beak, and of course, the single breast—he began to understand how a protected barbarian had survived and wandered freely on this space station rather than end up chained on the slave block.

The warrior cawed, "Did you find yourself a man finally?"

He didn't miss the sudden color in the barbarian's cheeks.

"I don't need a man!" she hotly declared.

"Then I guess it's a good thing you're adept at masturbation."

Thyos almost laughed at the Zonian's blunt words.

The Earth female turned so mottled he feared she might explode. "Shut your beak, Ishtara."

"Or what?" The Zonian warrior, with her vivid yellow gaze, leaned forward rapaciously as if daring the female to attack.

The human didn't cower. She leaned forward and snarled, "Don't tempt me to kill you. I'd hate to feel guilty about gutting a friend."

The threat had the one called Ishtara bellowing with laughter. "You, kill me? You always know how to amuse, Red Tide."

"Don't you start with that name again," the human grumbled.

Thyos listened in rapt attention to the strange repartee. It reminded him of the jesting among the warriors at home. Perhaps they weren't so different after all.

"You should accept the fine name given to you," the Zonian declared.

"I don't need a new name, because I have one. Clarabelle. Remember? Clar-a-belle." She enunciated slowly.

A strange series of consonants, too many in his mind. "Why Red Tide?" he found himself asking, drawing the Zonian's attention.

"Who are you?" Ishtara eyed him suspiciously.

Thyos knew better than to move too quickly. She'd attack at once if she thought him hostile. The Zonians were fast. Renowned. Deadly.

Their reputation closely mirrored that of his own people, meaning he would show her respect. Yet, at the same time, he was almost tempted to see what would happen if they did battle head to head. Was the rumor of their fierceness true or exaggerated? He wouldn't mind experiencing a taste. Good sparring partners weren't always easy to find.

Since he saw no harm in giving his name, he replied. "I am Thyos of—"

The Clara-a-belle interrupted. "His name must be

dumbass because only an idiot would interrupt me having a conversation with my friend."

"She asked me a question. It would be disrespectful to not reply."

"Only because you listened in on a private conversation," she reminded.

"And?" It was only eavesdropping if a person hid to listen.

"And my nickname is none of your business."

Why did her gaze slide to the side? Why was she turning an interesting shade of red?

"Red Tide is unique. I assume you earned it?" He could only imagine what it meant. "Is it because of how you use your knives in a fight?"

Ishtara snorted. "She wishes! Girl bleeds like she's going to die when her woman's time hits. Messy and avoidable if she'd just agree to a few stitches."

"Oh, my gawd, what is wrong with you?" Belle—he decided on a much more manageable version of her name—yelled. "I cannot believe you just told him about my periods."

"I don't understand your embarrassment of female menses." Ishtara sniffed. "It is quite common among the lesser races. Not us, of course. We have perfected the art of procreation."

According to biology literature on the procreation practices of Zonians, that involved an egg, a warm and bloody corpse, and a bed of coals. Add some seasoning and it sounded like dinner to him.

Belle gritted her teeth and hissed, "You know we don't talk about that stuff."

"You don't, and it is a weakness. Embrace the fact

you're a copious bleeder. Perhaps a male will think it makes you an excellent breeder, thus increasing the possibilities of fertilization."

"Ewww." Belle's embarrassment was clear and amusing.

But it also brought up a concern for him. "Do you not wish to create progeny?"

"Not particularly." Her nose wrinkled.

"She says that now," Ishtara interrupted, "and yet you put a screaming, wrinkled, fleshy blob in her arms and she'll change her mind."

Thyos couldn't stop his laughter at Belle's expression, which only deepened her scowl. "Perhaps I can aid in her finding an appropriate donor."

"I don't need your help. As a matter of fact, you can leave now." She thought she could dismiss him.

As if. He'd just found her. He wasn't about to leave.

He got his chance when the Zonian asked, "How can you help?"

Belle hastily huffed, "He can't. He doesn't know of any humans. I'm the first he's met."

Ishtara eyed him. "Can you find more humans?"

This was a direct question, and lying here would get him hurt later, so he hedged. "Maybe."

"First it's he can, now it's maybe," Belle drawled. "He's lying and wasting our time."

"I'm not lying." He looked her straight in the eye as he said, "I can give you what you need."

Ishtara clicked her beak. "He's telling the truth as he knows it."

"He's obviously deranged." Belle glanced at him and

with a sneer said, "Exactly how many times were you dropped on your head as a child?"

"None."

"Which explains the soft skulls," Ishtara clucked. "For me, I was dropped several times during the formative stage."

"You're kidding, right?" Belle asked.

"Why would I jest? It's a common practice to strengthen the textile thickness of a skull with some well-applied blows," Ishtara replied.

"You do realize you're just causing hematomas that lead to permanent brain damage, right?" Clarabelle asked.

"Not true," the Zonian scoffed. "My head can withstand most direct blows without any ill effect. Why, I've been whacked more than a hundred times and look at me. I'm stronger than ever." Ishtara thumped her chest.

"Do you remember what you did in that bar last night after you rode the bucking Trewrm?"

Judging by the frown on Ishtara's face, she didn't.

Clarabelle leaned close and whispered, loud enough he could hear, "Picture this if you can. You and an Ymp in a bar, humping on the dance floor."

The statement led to the Zonian clucking and the stubby wings on her back snapping. "You lie."

"Am I? Have you taken a pregnancy test in the last day?"

"I would know if I fornicated."

"If you remembered..." The human female blinked in false innocence.

He almost laughed. The banter proved wildly entertaining.

"One day someone will slit your throat while you sleep. You are truly evil," grumbled Ishtara, only to beam. "I'm so proud."

"Only because I had an awesome teacher." The pair grinned at each other, and that quickly, the verbal sparring stopped and they both turned their attention on him.

"What should we do about him?" Belle asked.

"Think he tastes any good?"

"I wouldn't suggest taking a bite," he warned. Perhaps he would get to fight, after all. The question being, should he overpower his mate or kill her in the hopes of finding a new one? Karma might punish him if he did the latter.

"Do you really think you can locate more humans for Red Tide and the others?" Ishtara demanded.

"Maybe. I can begin seeking immediately," he hastened to add, as those wings on the Zonian's back extended in agitation.

"What makes you think you'll find anything? I've been looking and looking and coming up empty," stated Clarabelle. "You'd think with a universe worth of information we'd get a kickass internet and search engine. But no. Finding out anything sucks ass because all you get are commercials. If I say search for a human, the first thing that comes up is dolls. Robotic, human-looking sex dolls!"

Ishtara took on a somber expression. "I've told you to be careful with those. There have been issues with some of those robots gaining sentience."

Even Thyos had heard about those androids who suddenly killed their owners and escaped. No one understood why it kept happening but assumed a virus. All the more reason to never allow that kind of sentient technology near Qhryce.

"I have no interest in a life-size Ken doll." The expression didn't mean anything to Thyos. "The only thing I need is my handy-dandy bob."

"Bob?" he queried, a spurt of jealousy making it a bark.

Belle had a smirk as she said, "Battery operated boyfriend."

"I never understand why you play with plastic when you can capture yourself the real thing." Ishtara hiked her belt.

"Bob doesn't talk back," was Belle's sassy retort.

"Your companion is correct," he interjected. "Nothing can replace sex in the flesh." He held Belle's gaze and noticed color rising in her cheeks before she ducked her head.

"Then have at it, dude. I'll stick to my little friend."

"Little being the whole problem," muttered Ishtara. "But we digress. I am interested in your proposal to aid us in our search."

"We don't need help," Belle grumbled.

"Apparently we do. I do not understand. If he is willing to give us information, why do you not accept?" asked Ishtara.

"Because, in exchange for this info that doesn't yet exist, I'm supposed to interfere with his engagement."

"Facilitate," he corrected.

Her nose wrinkled. "I'd rather not convince some poor woman to marry you. If you're going to be cruel, then maybe it would be kinder to kill your fiancée rather than subject her to you."

The insult amused him. "Are you certain being mated to me would be horrifying?"

"I don't know. I've yet to see your face." She cocked her head and tried to peer in the shadow of his cowl, but he already knew she wouldn't see a thing. A slight mirage, projected by the tech woven into the fabric of his cloak, made him anonymous.

"Does appearance matter?"

"Yes." She didn't even hesitate.

"What of character?"

"That's important, too, but most people don't want to be hooking up with someone gross."

"What is this gross?" he asked.

"With her, anything that swings a dick apparently," Ishtara muttered.

"Don't you start again," Belle growled.

"I'll do whatever I like, little girl."

"Don't call me little!"

"Fine. Red. Tide." Each word was enunciated and meant to rile Belle.

Before they could truly try and murder each other, he said loud enough they would both hear, "Do we have a deal or not?"

"You know, it occurs to me that maybe instead of getting help from you, perhaps I should approach your fiancée. Find out how she feels about getting hitched to you," Belle sourly stated.

"I can save you the trouble. She'd be appalled."

"You mean she doesn't know?"

"Not yet," he said with a hint of a smirk.

"Then she won't miss you at all when I slit your throat and dump you in the freezer for dinner." Belle thumbed the hilt of a knife.

"I am beginning to think your companion is correct when she says you hate males."

"I don't hate men," she huffed.

"Says the female uttering death threats instead of being mature and striking a bargain," he countered.

"Ha! He just called you a whiny child." Ishtara snorted.

"This child is about to have an epic meltdown. I don't want your help."

"You might not want it, but you need it," Ishtara declared. "We can't keep wandering around aimlessly, looking for compatible males."

"I thought you sought a human settlement," he said.

Again, the Zonian made a disparaging sound. "She seems fixated on the idea of finding human males, but I say she shouldn't be so picky and should accept anything with a compatible penis. Even a deft tongue would solve the problem she and the other orphans are suffering."

"The problem being?" he asked, knowing the answer but wanting to see the explosion.

"Lust. The females are in heat and in need of some sexual relief."

"Oh, my gawd, I can't believe you're telling him this!" Clarabelle squealed.

"How is he supposed to find you compatible stock if you don't advise him of your requirements?"

No mistaking the heated color in her face. "I am not just looking to hook up with a guy. I want to have a home, a family, a life with people like me."

Did Clarabelle not see the sad tilt to Ishtara's features when she threw that statement?

"I know you do, which is why I'm here to help you find it." Ishtara switched from melancholic to rapier sharp as she zoned in on Thyos. "Can you truly help?"

"I can find her a compatible male," he insisted. He wasn't completely lying. After all, he hadn't specified that male would be human.

"I don't need you playing matchmaker." Belle wouldn't budge.

Ishtara ignored her. "How do we know you are trustworthy?"

"You don't." He shrugged. "But I would say me not attacking like those six in the alley would show some measure of respect."

"Six?" Ishtara swung her yellow gaze onto Clarabelle.

"Seven actually, but the first one was some random dude who thought he could grab my buttocks. He failed the worthiness test."

"And the other six?"

Clarabelle smirked as she said, "They all failed, too."

Knowing a bit about the Zonians and their mating rituals, he was aware that they often fought their males to see if they were worthy of their sexual attention. The idea of grappling with her oddly excited.

"How will you ever find acceptable males if you keep killing them?" Ishtara harangued.

"Would you feel better if I said I won't kill any human men we find?"

"What if they deserve it? Will you spare them simply based on their genetics?" Thyos interrupted.

She turned a green gaze on him. She sneered. "Don't tempt me to slit your throat."

"Go ahead and try," he taunted. Would she?

"Yes, go ahead," Ishtara exclaimed, clacking her beak in agitation. "Let's kill all the males we encounter. Picky chit."

"Don't blame me for having criteria."

"I will blame you for reducing our options. We are running out of places to look," the Zonian warrior grumbled.

"Which is why you need my help," he reminded.

"I don't—"

Ishtara slapped the palm of her clawed hand over Clarabelle's mouth. "We accept."

Clarabelle glared.

"Most excellent. If you would follow me back to my world, I can make inquiries."

The human ducked out of her companion's reach. "Follow you? Ha. As if that's not a trap." Her sarcasm dripped thickly.

It was not entirely misplaced. She was astute. He did have a trap of sort planned. "How else will you pay me when I succeed?"

"Are you saying I'd renege on the deal?" She prickled.

"You seem to think I would," he countered.

Ishtara slapped them both on the backs. "Children, keep in mind that only weaklings and cowards use traps."

The insult was so nicely given it took a moment. The Zonian had effectively boxed him in. Subterfuge in his actions would be seen as cowardly.

Which was why he stood straight and said, quite seriously, "The real reason I want you to join me on my home planet is so we might conduct the mating rites." At Belle's blank look, he kept talking. "There is no fiancée, no other woman. When I said I found my mate, I meant you, Belle. You're my *sykyrah*."

He waited for the anger. Kept an eye for a knife.

He got laughter.

Loud, throaty laughter as the human fell against her companion and gasped, "You are funny."

"I am simply stating the truth. You are my mate. Karma has decreed it. There is no escaping our fate."

Wiping at the moisture in her eyes, she straightened. "Dude, first off, I am not getting hitched to you. I don't care how many tea leaves you read or what your horoscope claims. Two, if I ever do decide to get hitched, the guy is gonna be human. Sorry. It's just something I feel is necessary. And three..." She eyed him. "You are way too big."

The two insults followed by a large compliment brought a smirk to his lips. "Your wants won't matter. A *sykyrah* bond isn't something that can be broken."

"The sic what?" She shook her head. "Listen, crazy dude, I am not getting married to you. Or sleeping with you."

He had to wonder if a resting period together had some meaning to an Earthling. Would it make the bond happen faster for her? Where was the nearest bed?

"Maybe you should give him a try," Ishtara suddenly said.

"Try what? Marrying the Grim Reaper? I don't even know if he has a face."

He lowered his hood finally and let her see him. His skin held a metallic bronze hint, his hair was dark, and his gaze strange, his eyes reptilian in many respects with their vertical slits. They also possessed a faint yellow glow.

She stared, but it was the Zonian who spoke. "He is not hideous."

Clarabelle glanced at him before shaking her head. "He's got freaky eyes."

"Do you think my eyes *freaky* as well?" Ishtara asked softly, startling the woman.

"Of course not. You're my sister." And he could see Belle meant it, though she still did not see how her words hurt.

"You're not exactly my type either," Thyos remarked and it wasn't just that her frame presented smaller than the women of his world. Her skin lacked the glint of bronze and gold and even iridescent green common among his kind. Not to mention her less-than-impressive posterior.

"You *wish* you could get someone as hot as me," she pertly retorted, thrusting out her chin and chest.

"Are you feverish?" Her temperature seemed normal, but what did he know of her kind?

"No, but I am sick of this conversation and you. Mate? Ha!"

Thyos found his patience waning. His pride was taking a beating, too. He'd done as told. He'd come looking for his mate. Just his luck, she wanted nothing to do with him.

Worse luck, he was more and more intrigued by her.

What to do?

On the one hand, he could probably arrange an abduction, knock her out via the use of narcotics and bring her to his planet. Given she'd probably wake annoyed, he'd have to hold her prisoner until she finally came to her senses and performed the ritual of bonding with him—sex on a seriously spiritual level.

For some reason, he didn't see this method succeeding. He did, however, see himself either dying young or acquiring some interesting new scars if he tried.

What other option remained?

She was his mate. The woman he needed to save his clan and the life tree. He tired of her arguing with everything he said, so he decided to put Karma to the test.

"Since you don't wish to make a bargain, then I'll take my leave. Best of luck." Without even a look back, he left.

He couldn't help wondering if he'd made a fatal mistake.

FIVE

"ABOUT TIME HE BUGGERED OFF," Clarabelle muttered, watching the cloak as it swirled around Thyos's frame as he marched away.

"What is that expression you like to use?" Ishtara mused aloud. "Another one bites the dust?"

That earned her friend a scowl. "He wasn't even close to being a contender."

"On account of his eyes. I heard," Ishtara muttered icily before turning on her hind claw.

In that moment, the insensitivity of her earlier remark hit her. "Oh shit. I'm sorry, Ish. I didn't mean I didn't like you. You know I adore you."

"I have yellow eyes."

She did, big glowing ones; whereas his were beady and mean and... Okay, he had gorgeous eyes and a metallic bronze cast to his skin. And an ego the size of a solar system.

"I'm an insensitive jerk who doesn't deserve to call herself your friend." She hugged Ishtara and leaned her head on the chest of the larger woman, baring her neck in a sign of trust.

Ish sighed. "You are irritating."

"But cute, right?" She grinned up at her friend.

"We should leave before someone takes offense at the bodies you've left littering the station," Ishtara grumbled.

"I'm sure some chef will be happy to recycle them." In the galaxies, where meat could oft times be limited, nothing was wasted. With the right spices, it tasted delicious.

It didn't take long to receive a window for departure. Only as they exited the space port did Ishtara ask, "Where to?"

Clarabelle bit her lip. She'd gotten no intelligence on the station, not even a rumor of a place to go. Just one annoying dude in a cloak. Who said he could help.

Yet left.

Obviously, he didn't mean it when he claimed they were soul mates. The very idea. It was—

"Where to?" Ishtara repeated.

For a moment, Clarabelle almost told her to follow his ship, but sanity affirmed itself, and instead, she said, "The next waystation. Let's talk to some more folks."

"Not giving up yet?"

"Never," she huffed.

Out there existed a home, a place to belong, and she was going to find it.

To Clarabelle's surprise and delight, they finally got a clue at their next stop. The news came from a purple dude with a dark, brooding appearance. He called himself Makl, the Galactic Avenger.

She'd never heard of him, but he had some interesting stories to tell about his supposed exploits. The one she enjoyed most was the rumor of a human outpost on a planet in an unclaimed star system. Makl even had vague coordinates for it that he sold to her for an astronomical sum.

"If this rumor is a trap, I will hunt you down, strip out your entrails, and feed them to you as you breathe your last," Clarabelle threatened.

Makl put a hand to his chest. "I can only look forward to the day we match wits and strength." Then he winked.

What did that mean? While his voice didn't make her shiver like Thyos's, she could admit maybe purple wasn't so bad. But bronze was nicer.

She shook her head and returned to the ship with the news.

"I've got a location!" She waved a jagged piece of parchment, expensive and yet still widely used. On Earth, paper was cheap and wasted on a horrendous level. In space, because electronics could be wiped, along with their data, many still chose to put to paper—or leather, or whatever they could write on—important things. Like coordinates. But actual paper could be difficult to find. And she currently held a fragile piece that was the equivalent of a space treasure map.

Ishtara eyed the squiggles and waggled the bony protuberance jutting past her eyes. "You bought this from a pirate?"

"He never claimed to be a pirate but some kind of galactic avenger."

"Of what?"

She shrugged. "He never said; I didn't ask."

"And on the basis of a rumor you spent how much?"

Never show uncertainty. She lifted her chin. "As much as needed to accomplish my task."

"Good girl." Ish nodded. "Let's see what these coordinates lead to."

Putting data into the computer wasn't a strong suit of hers. Clarabelle proved handy in other ways. She could weld and run electrical. Fix plumbing and mechanical stuff, but when it came to the actual instructions and numbers, she let the experts handle it.

"Hmm." Ish clicked her beak a few times.

"What is it?" she asked, leaning in to glance at a screen filled with symbols and lines that meant nothing to her.

"You're sure of those coordinates?"

"As sure as I can be of third-hand info. Why? What does the computer say?" Because Clarabelle couldn't understand any of it.

Ish inclined her beak toward the screen. "Nothing because the system it leads to is closed."

"Meaning what?"

"Meaning that information about its existence is restricted to inhabitants."

"People can do that?"

"Some races are more private than others and don't wish to advertise any weakness."

"Do you think they're human?"

"I know nothing." Ishtara shrugged.

"Meaning they might be." She smiled. "It would make sense. Why else keep it a secret?"

"There are many reasons to hide. You mustn't assume."

"Fine, I won't assume shit until we see it for

ourselves." But Clarabelle couldn't help the excitement as they travelled, and she wondered, had they finally found a home?

Her optimism fizzled when faced with reality. The moment they entered the protected star system, they encountered many planets, all of them appearing barren of intelligent life. Not a single projecting satellite or guard ship. Their communication system remained silent. Proof that only the most rustic of outposts existed in this galaxy or the silence before the spring of a trap?

What if it were simply because there wasn't anything to find?

"I think you were sold some bad information," Ishtara claimed.

Hard to disagree. Clarabelle watched the screen that provided a live video feed of the world they orbited. The planet indicated on her map.

It appeared barren of civilization. Definitely no visible buildings or even a basic spaceport. The coordinates led to a cleared section on the surface, really nothing more than a thin scar of short, scrubby grass amidst a blanketing green forest. From above, the giant blue lakes—massive enough to be called seas—were bordered by green and brown, trees and dirt, with a single sun in the sky. She couldn't help but swallow.

"What's wrong?" Ishtara immediately asked.

"This planet. It reminds me of Earth."

Her friend cocked her head and squinted. "Not really, unless you mean before the humans razed the forests and paved it over to build their cities. Given the pristine state of this planet, I predict there are no humans in the vicinity."

"That's mean."

"But true. Civilization tends to leave its mark."

"Unless they've learned to live in harmony with their environment." Not many species ever evolved to that extent. Even the Zonians had a tendency of razing areas to the ground for their villages.

"I think we made the voyage for nothing." Ishtara pored over her screens, looking for signs of anything.

"Maybe what we seek is hidden for safety."

"More likely it's a trap."

"Do you really think that?" She took her gaze from the planet to scan the space around them, keeping special watch on the orbiting moons that might hide enemies.

"Wouldn't that be lovely?" Ishtara enthused at the prospect.

Zonians craved battle and confrontation. Thrived on chaos. Clarabelle didn't mind, and yet it would be nice to not always have to hunt down her dinner or fight to keep her place. To return to a normal way of living like she used to enjoy.

"No smoke signs. No communications chatter." Ish kept monitoring for any evidence of civilization.

"Could be they are underground?"

"Why would they live below the ground given the air is a perfect blend suitable for human lungs?"

Ish had already studied air quality and would probably test the foliage and local wildlife next. Clarabelle had a feeling it would be compatible as well.

"I didn't say they *did* live underground, just mentioned it as a possibility."

"I still don't understand why. It doesn't sound pleasant."

Clarabelle's nose wrinkled. "No, it doesn't. I kind of hoped I'd live somewhere sunny."

Looking upon the verdant world, she almost stated, "I've come home." This planet was the closest she'd come to feeling as if she were back on Earth.

They landed in the strip of grass without fanfare. No one came to greet them, guns didn't rise from the ground via hidden turrets to target, and sirens didn't scream to noisy life.

Stepping out of the ship, she couldn't help but notice the silence was broken only by the ticking of their cooling engine parts. There was a slight rustle of grass as a light breeze sluiced through it and the trill of an animal. Bird, rat, bear... Who cared? There was life here.

Fresh air. She breathed deep.

"Not a very appealing locale," Ishtara grumbled, stomping past. "All that green and whoever heard of a blue sky?"

The reminder had Clarabelle tilting her head back and smiling at the sight of it. The sun wasn't a yellow ball, but the white, fiery nature of it was close.

"I like it." She really did. "Shall we split up to see if we can find a settlement?" Because that was the only thing that could make this planet even more perfect.

"How long shall we search before admitting defeat?" Ishtara asked, slinging a large harness with a sheathed sword around her torso.

"Could we at least try to be a little positive?"

"I don't like to lie."

Clarabelle loved and hated that about her friend.

"Then how about you say nothing at all. Meet you back here by sunset."

They set off in opposite directions, armed for danger, and each sporting a communication device. Not to call for help. Ishtara would bleed out before she'd admit she needed any.

Clarabelle was proud but did have a thing about living. If that made her a coward, then she would at least be kicking around to bask in the shame of it.

The field proved odd. The grass appeared trimmed, the area clear of any bushes or saplings, as if weeded. The question being, who maintained it?

It didn't take long to cross the field and reach the tree line. The trees towered a good twenty feet overhead. She'd yet to see any signs of life or habitation. The ground remained free of trails.

But then again...when she looked back, she couldn't even see where she'd traversed. Could it be the planet didn't allow any permanent paths?

As she stepped into the shade of the forest, Clarabelle kept a tight grip on her knife. Under the boughs forming a dense canopy, the leaves filtered the sunlight, placing her in a pale shadow. She finally caught movement as insects flitted past, their wings a blur of color, the rapid rub of them humming.

She stepped carefully, knowing how to place her feet so that she didn't make a sound. All her senses were tuned to the forest. And still, she only barely realized she wasn't alone.

At the realization, she whirled and saw a figure standing not far off between two trees. She flung her dagger end over tip and gaped as it was caught by the hilt.

Midair.

Impressive.

"I believe this is yours." The cloaked stranger held it out.

Rather than snatch it, she reacted to the familiar deep voice. "You! Why are you stalking me?" More importantly, why did her heart race?

"I would ask the same of you. This is my world. You are the one following it seems."

"You live here?" she said slowly.

"Yes." Thyos shoved back his hood and revealed his very handsome face cut with a square jaw. A hint of a smile curved his lips. Pity he had less-than-human eyes. Looking into them gave her shivers.

"I don't believe you."

"Why would I lie?"

She swept a hand to encompass the forest around them. "Because this isn't the advanced planet of some alien race who can gallivant around space. It's too virgin."

"There is more to my world than you can see."

"Says you."

"Yes, says me. Would you like to see some of it?"

There had to be a trap in there somewhere.

Trap...

She jabbed a finger in his direction. "You made me come here."

"How exactly did I force you? I did not abduct you, although I could have. Nor did I threaten you or your companion. On the contrary, I left and returned home. *You*," he stressed, "are intruding on my space."

"Ha. Intruding on what?" Again, she gestured to the forest around him. "You going to claim all this land?"

"Not this section, no. The area around the landing fields is neutral grounds accessed by several tribes."

"So that grassy field is intentional. Do you use sheep to keep it mowed down?" she sassed.

"Sheep." He mulled the word aloud. "That is an animal providing components for fabric building and food on your world."

She blinked. "How do you know that?"

"I've been studying your kind."

The knowledge startled. "Why?"

"Because I was curious."

If he had to do research, then that could only mean one thing. "I'm going to go out on a limb and say there are no humans here."

"There is one."

Given he stared in her direction, she knew who he meant.

"Bloody hell. Ish is going to kill me."

"I'm confident you would prevail in a fight, and if not, our medical units are quite adept at reattaching limbs, although we've had lesser success with heads."

Startled by the statement, she eyed him then realized he took her literally again. Rather than correct him, she found herself asking, "Have you come to your senses regarding that fated mate thing?"

"Would I have gone through the effort of bringing you here otherwise?"

In that moment, realization slapped her. She eyed him suspiciously and said sourly, "That information given to me by the purple dude. Makl. You bribed him to lie, didn't you?"

"I told you fate would bring us together."

"Paying someone to feed me false information isn't fate," she argued. "I thought you said you didn't make me come here."

"I didn't. Merely started a rumor that you chose to believe."

She glared. "You're splitting hairs."

"Why would anyone do that? It seems rather useless and detrimental."

"It's an expression. It means— You know what, never mind what it means. You seeded that rumor on purpose, knowing I'd hear it and come looking."

"Don't be angry because I outmaneuvered you."

"Trapped me!"

He gestured to the forest at her back. "You may leave at any time. I won't stop you."

"Won't stop me?" She snorted. "Kind of hard to do anything with your guts on the ground."

"I don't think you'll kill me," he stated with too much confidence.

Given he still held her knife, she snatched it and played with the sharp edge. "Maybe I'll maim you instead."

Why did her threats make him smile?

"You have a fierce spirit. You'll need it if you're going to get my tribe to accept you."

"I don't give a rat's ass what your tribe wants. We are not hooking up."

"The sooner you accept we are *sykyrah*, the better."

"Dude, did no one ever teach you ultimatums don't work? I am not going to be your wife."

"Are you always this obstinate when faced with facts?"

"Are you always this annoying?" she grumbled.

"Only when I'm right." He dared show a dimple when he said it.

She ignored the cuteness of it. "I can't believe you wasted my time bringing me here." She rubbed a hand through her hair.

"How did I waste it? You are seeking a world with possible mates for you and your sisters." He spread his hands, the seam of his cloak opening to show two legs, two arms, and a thick body that appeared to have no fat, just lots and lots of muscle. "I have done as promised."

"I asked for humans. Not"—she waved her hand—"whatever you are." A part of her realized how awful she sounded, and yet the words still rolled off her tongue.

"I am Spa'Rtk'un," he declared, flinging off his cloak.

She blinked once, then twice, before turning on her heel to march back to her ship. Of course, he just had to follow.

"Your resistance is futile," he declared.

"According to you," she snapped. "I am not about to give in. You and I will never happen. Ever."

"Why not?"

She whirled and pointed. "Because you have a freaking tail."

SIX

BELLE DIDN'T POINT out the obvious with awe but rather disgust. It prickled.

"Don't be jealous just because your own posterior is lacking," Thyos declared.

"My ass is perfect."

"I assume you are referring to your buttocks and not a hairy, ornery animal," he asked, as his translator offered two choices.

"Does your translator not handle slang?"

"Your language will require an update apparently since many of your expressions don't translate well." His tail flicked side to side, and she paled, even took a step away from him.

Rather than hide, he slid the tip closer. He refused to be shamed by a tail he took pride in, the muscle of it firm, the exterior bronze scales and the tip flexible enough to grip.

"Stop that!"

"Stop what exactly?" he goaded.

"That thing with your tail. Keep it away from me."

"It really bothers you," he stated.

"It's weird."

"More like you are intolerant."

"Did you just call me racist?" She blinked at him. Surprised obviously. How could she not realize how her own words condemned her?

"You are reacting because of an inherent bias against those who are different than you."

"Hell yeah I'm reacting. In case you don't know it, you're an alien."

"So are you, or do you think there aren't things that I find odd about your appearance as well?" he countered. Did she not grasp how different she appeared to him? Not bad or ugly, but very different. However, at the same time, he thought her beautiful for her uniqueness.

She obviously didn't see him in the same manner. It bothered because more than ever he knew she was his *sykyrah*. Fighting it when it shone so obviously was pointless. Still, he couldn't help the disappointment at being saddled with a female who thought him repulsive.

Would she ever come to look on him favorably?

"I have no problem with you finding me ugly," she declared, her chin tilted upward.

"But that's just it, I don't. You are very attractive to me."

The various expressions on her face had him tucking his hands behind his back, waiting for her to settle on a stubborn cast where her lower lip jutted.

"You're just saying that to get in my pants. Don't think I'm going to give in to your brainwashing about me being your soulmate something or other. That would be impossible given we're not even the same species. Shouldn't you be sniffing after a chick of your own kind?"

"I would rather, actually," he growled, wondering why he bothered talking to the woman. She didn't want to even try. "But what I want and what you want don't matter. The goddess has spoken. Fate will have its way."

"Are you for real? Goddesses and fate? You can't tell me you actually believe in that shit. Free will, dude. We're all born with it. At least I was. I don't know about you." Her retort was accompanied by an interesting roll of her eyes, the disdainful gesture one he recognized. In many ways they weren't as different as she thought.

"I have freedom and choice in almost everything; however, this is more than choice. This is fate. It knows what we need, better than you or me," he said softly.

She stared at him and then laughed. "Holy crap, what a load of bull. You can't seriously expect me to swallow that."

He didn't know what possessed him to say, "You don't have to swallow. Spitting is fine."

The taunt rendered her almost speechless. "Pig!"

That was an insult he understood. She compared him to the ugly porcine pirates. It brought a smile to his lips.

"Did you know my research shows the copulation between our species is remarkably similar?" He didn't mean for it to be provocative, yet her gaze dipped.

He hardened because she looked. It was shocking and exciting and annoying all at once. Frustrating, too, as she declared, "There will be no sex."

"Are you a virgin?"

The redness in her cheeks proved even more vivid

than her hair. "Would you stop that? My sex life is none of your business."

"It will be. Feel free to tell me what you like done. Or don't..." He grinned widely. "I can experiment until I discover what you enjoy."

She practically exploded. "Don't you dare touch me."

"Until you ask for it. Agreed."

"Excuse me but I wasn't conducting a bargain. And I don't appreciate you harassing me."

He took on a patient tone as he said, "I am discussing it with you. If you don't want to talk about how you'll be tearing stripes into my back, then we can change the subject."

"Hell yes. Change the subject."

"What would you prefer to discuss?"

"How about the fact that you seem intelligent until you open your mouth and claim to believe in a god?"

"Goddess," he corrected. "Karma, the embodiment of chance."

"I guess you're not a good disciple given your bad luck."

"Bad how? I set out to find my *sykyrah*, and here you are." He knew it would annoy her. He was right.

She stamped her foot. "I thought you said you would stop."

"Talking about sex. This is fate and Karma's will."

"You should think about switching religions," she growled. "Maybe find a new god or goddess who lets you make your own choices. Wouldn't you like to fall in love the proper way?"

"Are you saying I haven't?"

For a moment she gaped at him before sputtering, "How can you love a stranger?"

She asked an interesting question, which meant it deserved a well-reasoned reply. "Strangers only when it comes to cognitive elements. The understanding of personalities is something that takes time, conversation, and experiences created together. But that covers only the emotional aspect. Chemically, a proper match occurs upon meeting, instantaneously without need of words or even actions."

"Fancy words don't make it science."

"Actually, they do, because we have the studies to prove the existence of a *sykyrah* bond. Do you think you're the first skeptic?" There was a time when his people used to fight the *sykyrah*, wondering why they had to obey, especially when the bond struck between a pair belonging to warring tribes.

"Are you trying to tell me that people have managed to dissect these so-called matings? How?" she snorted. "Did they send out a survey and say hey, are you happy in your arranged marriage?"

"No need to have couples submit anything given a *sykyrah* bond is very noticeable, not to mention measurable on a few scales."

"And because of some tests you're going to claim instant love between people who never met before?" she challenged.

"That's how it happens most often. The turning of a corner, the sudden meeting of eyes."

"Then what? Lightning bolt?"

"It's a jolt of something. It's hard to explain." He shrugged.

"But you felt it? With me?" she specified, making it obvious she hadn't experienced the same.

"We wouldn't be talking otherwise."

"It's one-sided only," she stressed. "I don't feel a thing."

"You will," he said with assurance.

Her lips flattened. "These sudden bonds, how many of them are successful long term? Do you have a lot of divorce?"

The definition was a foreign concept. "There is no dissolution of a *sykyrah* bond, ever."

"What if the hubby turns out to be an abusive drunk? Or the wife cheats?"

"A mated pair would never harm each other."

"If that's true, then why do I want to slit your throat?"

"Want and do are two mightily different things." He didn't worry given she'd sheathed her knives. "I'm sure in time I'll make you content enough you'll just want to strangle me."

"As if I'd ever be content," she huffed, only to quickly correct herself by saying, "We'd never work."

"Then we'd be one of the few couples to fail."

"I thought you said there was no divorce."

"There isn't. The couples who fail simply aren't *sykyrah* anymore."

"Meaning what, instant annulment?"

"Call it as you wish. It's rare and considered quite shameful."

"How is it shameful? It's practically an arranged marriage. Surely not every single couple is happy. That's impossible," she sputtered.

"The whole point of a *sykyrah* bond is the perfect meshing. Why would anyone be unhappy?"

"But how do you measure happiness?" she asked.

"You can see it. Feel it. The mating bond brings a feeling of wholeness."

"I really hope you don't think everything you're saying is going to convince me to drop my pants, open my arms, and say, 'Make me yours.'"

Her method of speaking took a bit of effort to understand as she implied things using different combinations of words. "It wasn't meant to do anything but to provide replies to some of your queries."

"I'm going to tell you right now that you and I"—she circled a finger to encompass them—"will be one of those that fail."

"What makes you believe that?"

"Because I don't like you."

Not entirely true. He could read her scent, lacking any fear but hinting of intrigue. See it in her body language, as she was relaxed and even slightly provocative with her hip tilt and shoulders back. "Who said you had to like me? We are *sykyrah*."

She gaped at him. "That doesn't sound very romantic."

The word filled his head with a meaning he didn't entirely grasp. It defined it as intimate gestures toward a mate or person of interest meant to soften their emotions and even entice into copulation.

It was an entirely foreign concept in some respects, mostly because the expectations behind it were just something that occurred naturally between mated couples. Part of the magic of finding a mate.

"The bond is more than romance or love. It is about balance and complementing."

"You want someone to tell you how wonderful you are?" she drawled sarcastically.

He shook his head. "You are mistaken. I don't mean to give praise. A truly mated pair are like two distinct pieces that interlock together to form something better."

"You've just described soulmates."

"Yes." This was a term he understood.

"Is that why you are so keen on finding yours?" She eyed him, and her lips pursed. "You know, if I ignore the tail and eyes, you're a good-looking guy."

"Your praise overwhelms," was his dry reply.

"Just meaning you should be able to find a chick that isn't me."

"There will be no other females. You are the one for me." It might have emerged a tad more ominous than expected.

Belle sure reacted as if it were a threat. She wagged a finger. "I am not the other piece to your puzzle, dude. You and I are like oil and water."

An expression he understood. "Even oil and water can be frothed to make something light and new." His tail weaved and drew her gaze.

She stiffened. "This has been interesting, but I need to go." She turned to walk away.

"Wait."

"Done talking."

He could tell she meant it, her back ramrod straight as she marched. He couldn't let her leave. Not yet. Not until she felt it, too, the madness within that wanted him to touch her and be with her.

"I would strike a bargain with you."

She kept walking, not even deigning to reply.

In the silence, he knew she couldn't miss hearing his next claim. "I know where there is a human settlement."

It caught her attention, and she whirled. "Where?"

"I will tell you where but only if you give me a chance to prove we are mates."

"You want sexual favors in exchange for a coordinate?" Her nose wrinkled. "No thanks."

"No coitus required. What I want from you are eight days spent in my company."

"Doing what?"

"Getting to know each other."

"Don't you mean convincing me I should ride the lizard and promise to be your wifey poo?"

His lips quirked. "I have no idea what you just said; however, I am going to assume it was rude and counter with, what are you afraid of?"

"I fear nothing, especially not you. But I want to know what happens at the end of those eight days. What if I still hate you?"

"If you still want to leave, then I will give you the coordinates to the human settlement."

"You'd let me leave?" The query emerged dubious.

"I won't force you." He trusted in fate even if Karma could be obtuse about it.

"How do I know you're not shitting me about knowing where a colony is?"

He surmised what she meant. "I have no reason to lie when I can prove my claim. I began searching for more of your kind the moment we parted." He held out his palm, and a light shone from it, coalescing into a hologram. The colors went from fuzzy to crisp.

It caught her attention, and she stared at the video footage of a town.

Her lips parted. "It looks so much like Earth, except the coloring is wrong. Orange instead of green grass. And those look like rocks but made of some kind of smoky glass." She appeared fascinated as she studied the mishmash of materials and styles of the buildings, but her true interest sharpened when she noticed the inhabitants.

"Are those humans?" She reached out to touch, only to disperse the image.

"Yes, and by all indications, they are from your planet Earth. Most are second and third generation with little recollection of your world other than stories passed down by the first wave of settlers."

"Tell me where it is."

"Eight days," he repeated.

The glare in her gaze would have incinerated him if she were from the Draegz world. "You won't get me to love you in eight days."

"Maybe not, but I predict we will be intimate."

Her laughter proved bright and shining. "I am not going to screw you."

This time he understood her slang. "You will. And enjoy it."

Her good humor faded. "Rape me and die."

"I won't force you to do anything. I will wait for you to seduce me."

Her expression clearly expressed her belief that she'd never be the one to initiate. He understood that feeling.

Given her intense repulsion of him, he'd be stubborn if pressed to seduce, too.

There was fate and then his situation. Perhaps she was right and they would be in that small percentage that failed. Somehow, he doubted that Karma would allow that to happen.

"Well, look at that, the planet isn't a lifeless waste of time after all." Ishtara's voice sounded entirely too bright.

Immediately suspicious, Clarabelle glanced at her friend. "You knew he'd be here."

"Suspected, yes. Our notes on this galaxy did mention a race of beings with bronze-colored skin, Serpion origin in nature."

"It is said the serpent God and our goddess Karma lay together and birthed a race that combined their best traits," he declared, reciting one of the many theories of their evolution.

"I should have known you were a snake the first time I met you." Belle scowled.

Did she not know how attractive she was despite it? It surprised him to find her paleness not as shocking as before. To him at least. When he presented her to his tribe, though, there would be much complaint. Marriage outside their species didn't happen often. It wasn't banned as such, more just they tended to be a solitary race. They had no interest in the affairs of others.

"Do we have a bargain?" he asked.

"A deal to do what?" Ishtara quickly asked.

"He knows where I can find a human settlement, but he won't give me the coordinates until I spend eight days with him."

Ishtara nodded. "Eight days should be enough time for him to plant a warrior babe in your belly."

He had to bite his inner cheek lest he laugh at Clarabelle's expression.

"We are not screwing!"

"I should hope not. Spinning around is likely to confuse his already less intelligent sperm. With your kind, it's best if you maintain a single position," Ishtara replied with sage advice and a nod. "On your back seems most productive, with your legs held in the air above your head after for maximum effect, allowing the seed to travel more easily to implant your womb."

"We are not talking about this." And then Belle did the oddest thing. She stuck her fingers into her ears and hummed loudly.

"What is she doing?" he asked the Zonian.

"Ignoring me. So let us discuss my accommodations, given we'll be here for at least eight days."

Clarabelle chose to hear that. "You can't tell me you're agreeing to this ridiculous deal."

"Sounds reasonable to me."

"It's blackmail."

"It's a business transaction," Ishtara corrected. "He gets something, you get something. I fail to see the issue."

He knew just the thing to goad her. "It's because she is already fighting her attraction for me and fears I am right when I tell her we are meant to be mates."

"Why would she fear mating with you?"

"I am well endowed," he declared in all seriousness.

Ishtara nodded. "My research says her kind like them large. And lubricated. I have creams if needed."

"I'm sure we'll manage," he choked out.

Clarabelle ground her teeth. "I hate you both." She stomped in the direction of her ship.

"Is she leaving?" he asked.

"Having a tantrum. She'll come around. According to the other orphans, the redheaded humans are known for their fiery tempers."

Was it the wrong time to wonder if that would extend to passion as well?

SEVEN

CLARABELLE PACED INSIDE THE SHIP. She didn't want to stay on this planet, but at the same time, she did need to prove a point to him and nothing more.

Soulmates indeed. The guy had a freaking tail. And glowing eyes. And broad shoulders. Did he have wings, too? She'd not yet seen his back. The lack of lumps under his cloak seemed to indicate a flat surface, but the same cloak had also hidden the tail.

As if she'd ever hook up with a guy sporting extra body parts. She knew some of the orphans were okay with it, but she found herself averse with no clear reason why.

Perhaps she should try and look past her prejudice to see the man and not the tail. Would the appendage between his legs be as expected or shocking? He claimed it was big. How big? He'd probably show her if she asked.

She shook her head to dispel the thought.

"Are you done sulking?" Ishtara's voice broke through her mental pacing.

"No, as a matter of fact, I'm not. How could you?" she said, whirling to face Ishtara.

"Not tell you possibility the planet was inhabited by non-humans?" Ishtara shrugged. "You would have said no."

That actually wasn't what she'd been about to ask. "Is that why you took his side instead of mine?"

"I do not understand your irritation. Our quest was to find compatible companions for you and the other orphans."

"Human ones!"

"Which, as you've discovered, is harder than you thought."

"They exist," she said, her lower lip jutting.

"Yes, and he is the one with their location. Meaning you need to stop whining about the deal you've struck and make the most of it."

"I am not whining. I don't like being forced."

"Then we leave. I will prep the ship." Ishtara moved from the doorway.

It took her a moment to yell, "Don't."

Her friend hadn't gone far. Ish peered around the jamb. "Yessss?"

The petulance shone in Clarabelle's reply as she said, "I'll give him his eight bloody days."

"Was that so difficult?" Ishtara asked.

"It's—" The ship jolted. Clarabelle's eyes widened. "What's happening?"

"The Spa'Rtk'un don't allow surface vehicles to sit for long. They're parking us in one of their underground hangars."

Trapping them.

Since Ishtara didn't seem worried, Clarabelle feigned nonchalance as well.

"Do you know where we'll be staying?" she asked.

"I'll be remaining aboard the ship, monitoring the repairs Thyos has offered to have made."

"You make it sound as if I won't be."

"Your bargain is to spend your time with him."

"Alone?"

Clarabelle probably deserved the snorted, "Is that fear I smell?"

She threw back her shoulders. "If he thinks I'm going to spread my legs for him…" She had a knife that would solve that problem.

She packed a rucksack of clothes, a few weapons, and a scanner to check all food and drink for narcotics. Last thing she needed was to be roofied and wake up with morning-after regret. As for booze, she'd steer clear of it.

The ship jolted a few more times before it stilled. When it appeared to be done moving, she took a deep breath and made her way to the exit chamber. There was hissing as air pressurized and then clanking as the door unsealed, opening to reveal the inside of a building. The ramp slid down, and as she exited the ship, she found herself in a more modern space than expected.

When Ishtara said underground, she'd assumed it would be a cave with rock and dirt walls. Instead, much like the Zonians' advanced caverns, it looked as if she were in some kind of concrete bunker with crisp lines and smooth floors, all of it a pale, clean gray. The vast space acted as a hangar for ships. There were two aside from their vessel, each several times their size. But no little orange guys fixing them.

How advanced were Thyos and his people? Unlike the primitive forest outside, this space appeared quite up to date and high tech.

There appeared to be no one around, and she craned with curiosity, counting doorways and noticing a lack of windows. Would she be given a cell without a view for her stay? Would he insist they share a room? A bed...

Her fingers fisted around the hilt of a dagger.

"Ready to kill me already?" His voice startled her.

The knife went flying hilt over tip. He casually leaned to the side, and it sailed harmlessly past.

He arched a brow. "Nervous?"

Yes, damn him. "Just checking your reflexes."

"Is this my warning that you plan to test me? Very well but expect to be tested in return."

Meaning what? Would he throw knives at her, too?

She took note of his attire, having paid it little heed before given her distraction with his tail. He wore a billowy shirt, open at the neck and tucked into a kilt that ended just past his knees. On his feet were sandals, not boots, the laces of them winding around his calves. His limbs, excluding the tail, appeared human if you ignored the fact they were a shiny bronze. Other than the tail, eyes, and skin color, was there anything else weird about him? She should have done a quick computer search to find out, especially since she knew his race.

Spa'Rtk'un. For some reason the word reminded her of Spartans back home. Dumb given they looked nothing alike, and yet the comparison stuck as they exited an elevator—where he appeared amused at her decision to remain silent—and emerged into a city of stone.

The people had her blinking in surprise. There were

bronzed folks, gold and copper, too, their bared skin gleaming and visible given many chose to wear solid-looking breastplates, metal armguards, and short leather kilts. Men and women alike held shields and a variety of swords and appeared to be practicing battle moves. "You let girls fight?"

"There is no letting," he retorted as he led her deeper into a village that might appear primitive, and yet that was only a façade. She'd seen the technology they wielded. "Unlike other races, the Spa'Rtk'un, and indeed all the tribes descended from our goddess Karma, know men and women are equal on the field of battle."

"You're going to claim equality of the sexes when you're Mr. Macho with me?" she queried.

"I don't understand."

She pursed her lips to think of a way to explain it. "You're very aggressive in your pursuit of me."

"Some would call it ardent."

"You're trying to tell me what to do."

"But not forcing you to do anything."

He had an answer for everything, but it was the feel of his hand on her arm, his warm, slightly calloused fingers on her skin, that flustered. She needed distraction. "Why all the weapons? Are you at war?"

"Just protecting ourselves."

"Speaking of protecting..." She glanced overhead at the sky that was so blue it almost white in places. "How come we never saw this city when we scanned the planet?"

"Because we know how to cloak our presence. No need for our enemies to so easily discern our location."

"Do you have a lot of enemies?"

"Not anymore." He grinned, and her heart skipped a beat.

She glanced away. "Where are we going?"

"To tackle the most arduous task first."

"Gonna have to be more specific, big guy. You've suggested plenty of things that I'm not looking forward to and plan to avoid."

He cast her an amused glance. "I can assure you anything you've thought of will be more pleasant than what comes next."

"Planning to torture me?"

"Worse. You're going to meet my mother."

EIGHT

HE SHOULD HAVE KNOWN she'd laugh.

"Holy shit, you're a mama's boy."

Thyos didn't grasp the meaning but assumed it was an insult. "You might wish to curb your mirth and more inflammatory remarks. My mother isn't going to be happy about your presence." Especially since he'd not given her any warning he'd found his *sykyrah*. A human.

"And do you always do what your mama tells you to do?" Clarabelle mocked.

"My mother only has my best interests at heart." But she would also be thinking of her own, how his mating with a barbarian would appear. That reminder had him saying, "She will probably try to kill you."

Belle coughed. "Seriously? And am I allowed to kill her back?"

"I'd prefer you didn't. My sisters might take offense."

"Sisters? How many do you have?"

"Too many," he grumbled. Three who'd somehow not

succumbed when the plague ripped through their planet decimating the female population.

"If they come after me, I will put them in their place," she warned.

"Do what you must. I can hardly blame my *sykyrah* for defending herself."

She blinked. "Hold on a second. Is your sudden interest in me solely because you want to rebel against your mommy?"

"No." He leaned down close to whisper by her ear. "I am interested because I think burying myself into you will be like finding nirvana."

She couldn't hide the heat flushing her body, and the scent of her... Oh, the scent told him everything he needed to know.

He kept walking, and it took her a moment to join him, silent and glancing at him. As they stood before his home, the grandness of it looming overhead, she tilted her head back. "This is where you live?"

"Yes.

"Jeezus, it's a freaking castle."

Having researched her kind, he understood why she would name it so. It sprawled with turrets and crenellations, but it was much more delicate than the blocky examples on Earth.

The door opened at their approach. Someone must have been watching.

He knew better than to try and stand in front of Belle, blocking any immediate danger. For one, she wouldn't appreciate it, and for another, his mother wouldn't respect Belle if she thought her too weak to defend herself.

Stepping over the threshold, she appeared interested in the architecture, which must have irritated his mother to no end, given she stood at the top of the staircase, hand on the hilt of her blade. Did Belle do so on purpose to not notice her? Or was she truly obliv—

Belle barely moved, and yet it was enough for the thrown dagger to sail harmlessly past. Despite the attack, she didn't look over her shoulder but rather pointed to the large piece of art hanging on the wall. "Pretty."

"A local artist painted it with the blood of the animals he caught in that very valley pictured." The reds were still vivid after all this time, and the use of the darker ochre from the wildlife provided texture and contrast.

"And the green?"

"Came from the flesh-based plants. I should mention it's not recommended you sleep in that valley at night unless you don't mind waking up as a pile of bones."

"I doubt I'll be here long enough to go exploring." She finally whirled but still ignored his mother, who glared.

"What is this?" his mother growled.

"Mother. How nice of you to be here." He smiled in the face of her laser glare.

"Of course, I'm here. I live here. Who is this?" No politeness in the barked query.

"My *sykyrah*," he declared and got to see his mother's nostrils flaring.

"But she's alien!" his mother huffed.

"That's what I said." Finally, Belle chose to acknowledge his mother's presence. "Trust me, I'm not keen on it either. Maybe you can talk some sense into him because he's all like, fate this, goddess that, and I'm like, dude, you and I"—she swirled a finger back and forth between them— "are from two different worlds."

"Very different," his mother stated, coming down the stairs. "What are you?"

"Human. And before you ask, no tail. No snake at all in my lineage."

"You appear weak."

"And your aim is shit," Belle said with a shrug.

"How dare you—"

His mother blinked as the knife soared too fast for either of them to move, slicing past her face, a single lock of hair drifting down to feather the floor.

"Let me know if you'd like lessons." Belle turned and strode off, peering into doorways, disappearing into the one for the food preparation area.

"She's rude," his mother huffed.

"Very."

"Talented with a knife, though."

The praise surprised him. "She was raised by Zonians."

"Really? How interesting," she mused aloud. "When is the bonding occurring?"

The rapid change had him blinking and looking for a reply. "I don't know."

"I'll need a few days, first to contact your sisters that they might return in time and also to prepare the party."

"Don't start planning yet. The bond might not happen."

"Excuse me? What did you say?" His mother turned to eye him, and he did his best not to fidget.

"Belle hasn't agreed yet."

"She is your *sykyrah*."

"Yes, but—"

"There is no but. It is fate."

"She doesn't believe in fate."

His mother was silent a moment then shook her head. "She can't escape it."

"Is that why you're not arguing about the fact she's not from our world?"

"Why would I argue? She's strong. And goddess chosen. Can you imagine the children you will have?"

His mother seemed too agreeable. Was she so desperate for him to settle down she'd truly accept Belle as his mate?

Then again, he'd come around quick enough to the idea. Seeing her again—smelling her and hearing her—he couldn't wait for her to become his bride.

NINE

CLARABELLE WOULDN'T HAVE ADMITTED it aloud, but Thyos had a really nice castle. House. Whatever he wanted to call it. It rocked with its nice things and big rooms. It had more than enough windows to let in sunshine with views of a green garden that she wanted to stroll. She felt so much at home that she even wondered for a moment if maybe staying wouldn't be so bad.

Sure, his mother had tried to kill her, but she understood that kind of aggression after being with the Zonians for a few years.

She had a prickling awareness she wasn't alone.

"You like the garden?" Thyos's voice came from behind her.

She ran her fingers over the soft leaves of a flowering plant. "It's beautiful."

"If there is a particular color you'd like to see, you just have to inform me, and I can have it ordered for planting."

"Isn't this your mother's domain?"

"My mother thinks it is a waste of time." He swept his hand. "She thinks I am odd for bringing home different clippings and making them grow."

The admission startled. "Wait, this is *your* garden?" She eyed him, this big warrior man who admitted to liking flowers.

"Growing plants is my hobby when I'm not doing other stuff."

"I don't have a hobby. Not anymore." On Earth, makeup, boys, and meeting up at the local fast food joint were her thing. The Zonians only believed in work. No play.

"In our society, it is recommended to have a pastime that is calming. Some choose to follow the culinary arts, others crafting or painting."

"And you grow flowers." She traced the delicate pink edge of a bloom that shivered. The incongruity of it had her whirling to face him. It was strange how she no longer saw his bronze skin as so different. Rather more exotic, especially against the lush backdrop.

What she liked less was the tingles she felt. Arousal for him, and after she'd said no sex.

"I am capable of many things." He purred the words, and she shivered.

To her surprise, they spent the day together as he performed his job as leader. He was respected by his people, who eyed her askance but said nothing.

He proved himself that day to be not only possessed of a green thumb but handy with tools as he helped with some repairs. Smart as he dealt with folks needing his input on supplies and the protection of what he called his tribe.

That evening she said, "People were eyeballing me."

"They're curious."

"Because I'm different."

"Yes." He didn't say anything, so she was forced to.

"But in many respects, we're not."

She eyed the remnants of the food on her plate. She didn't recognize it, but it tasted delicious. Of course, she didn't eat the plate his mother handed her. Rather she waited for Thyos to take a bite of his then reached over and swapped their dishes. When his mother didn't protest as he kept eating, she figured she was safe from poison. For now.

His mother said nothing during dinner, but she did stare a lot at Ishtara, who'd arrived with her usual stomping grace just as they were sitting down.

Ish wasn't one to let a foul-tempered mother bother her. "You overcooked the meat," Ish declared, wrinkling her beak. Given Zonians liked it raw for the most part, any kind of heat applied to it was too much.

"I agree," said Thyos, smirking in his mother's direction.

Which led to said woman standing and declaring, "Are you a barbarian who has no idea how food should be prepared?"

"Perhaps you should show me," Ishtara replied.

The next thing Clarabelle knew, Ish had joined Thyansa in the kitchen for an exchange of culinary techniques, leaving Clarabelle alone with Thyos.

Which shouldn't have mattered. She'd been with him all day, though mostly in the company of others. But there was something different about this, with the sunset, dim lighting, and her belly full.

When he rose and said, "Shall we go sit somewhere more comfortable?" she agreed and prepared herself to foil his next move. Because surely seduction would come next.

Instead, he grabbed a tablet from a low-slung table, indicated she could grab the other, and ignored her to read.

Or so she assumed, given when she slid her finger across the tablet screen, she was shown covers and titles that changed from gibberish to English when she pressed on one.

A book. She hadn't read one since her abduction from Earth.

Next thing she knew, she was leaning against the arm of the divan, feet up on the cushions, toes pressing on his thigh. It was the most relaxing thing she'd done in ages.

When he declared, "Bedtime," she only stirred slowly.

Was this when it would finally happen? The day but a sham for what he'd try next?

He led her up the stairs and pointed to a door. "Those are your quarters. See you in the morning."

He did nothing else. Didn't try to kiss her. Or ask her to join him. He simply went into the room across the hall and closed the door.

She stood, staring for a moment at the closed door. Waiting.

Annoyed with herself.

Annoyed with him.

Which might be why, when she wakened a while later after spending some time tossing and turning and heard the whispered, "I can break the *sykyrah* bond," she over-reacted.

TEN

IT WAS ONLY a squeak of sound, and yet Thyos woke instantly. Then paused to listen. Nothing marred the deep silence of night, and yet unease gnawed at him. It took a moment to discern why.

Belle!

He didn't pause to think, or dress. He crossed the hall and threw open the door to Belle's room. It remained mostly in shadow, but the hall light shone inside enough for him to see Belle sitting atop his sister Thyara, holding a knife at her throat.

Curse his meddling family. He should have known they'd made things too easy thus far. Still, to attack his *sykyrah* while she slept... He was almost tempted to leave his sister to her fate. But then he recalled how when she was a child she always held up chubby arms for him to lift her.

It caused him to utter a resigned, "Don't kill her."

His intended growled. "Give me a good reason why."

"Because she's my sister."

"She's in my room."

"Which is rude. I agree," he soothed softly. Inside, he silently raged. He'd thought his mother would be the worst hurdle, and yet his guilty sister was the one on the floor, intending what exactly? Murder?

"I just wanted to talk to her," Thyara groused. "She attacked me."

"You're lucky that's all she did. What were you thinking?"

"Can't you guess? She doesn't think I'm good enough for you," Belle snapped.

"The goddess wouldn't shame our family by mixing it with the blood of an outsider," Thyara insisted.

"Are you sure?" he asked. "Because I have spoken to Karma, and she was rather insistent that my *sykyrah* wouldn't come from our world or even our star system."

"You guys and your stupid goddess." Belle shoved off of Thyara to her feet, but she didn't sheathe her knife.

"Do not blaspheme the goddess!" Thyara sounded most shocked.

"Your goddess can—"

He ushered his sister out before Belle could finish the insult then shut the door and leaned on it. "My apologies your rest was interrupted."

"It's like being at home. The Zonians have this thing about making sure we can act the moment we're wakened so they drill us all the time for preparation." For some reason she sounded weary as she said it.

A few things occurred to him in that moment. The first and foremost being that the main reason she wanted to find a human settlement wasn't just for the species factor but because she wanted a life that was more than just being constantly ready for battle. It would be hard to convince her that the life in his tribe would be calm most of the time, given that, since her arrival, two of his family members had attacked her.

"Our village is safe." For now, at any rate. There was no honor in attacking a failing tribe.

"From outsiders, maybe, but apparently it's the inhabitants I have to watch for."

"I am sorry for my sister's actions."

"Are you?" Belle finally put her knife away, but what he liked less was she went for the pile of clothes on the chair and began to dress. He wouldn't have minded her remaining a moment longer in the slim fitting shorts and cropped top that outlined her lean physique.

"Do not confuse her feelings with mine."

"She wants me gone."

"I don't."

"I'm not about to live somewhere I have to watch my back all the time."

"If you became my *sykyrah*, they wouldn't dare harm you."

Clarabelle snorted. "I'm not worried about me. But if you're attached to them, it could get dicey." She slid on her boots.

"Are you going for a walk?"

"You might say. Listen, this isn't going to work. Might as well face it now. We couldn't last one day together, let alone a lifetime."

"You said you'd give me eight days."

"You might not have any family left by the end of it," was her ominous proclamation. "Best for us both if I leave."

Leave? She couldn't go. Not yet. He had to do something. "What if you didn't have to deal with my family?"

"Going to murder them yourself?" was her sardonic reply.

"More like going to suggest we escape them for a bit. How do you feel about camping in the wild?"

ELEVEN

WHAT HAD POSSESSED her to say yes? Clarabelle wasn't a person who enjoyed shitting in the woods or sleeping on the ground, yet the thought of being alone with Thyos enticed.

It shouldn't have.

She'd been ready to leave. Being constantly on her guard didn't appeal. Screw seven more days of vigilance. Yet despite all the reasons to go, she found herself riding a hover bike of some kind out into the wilderness. The bike made her think of the ones used in that *Star Wars* movie she'd watched as a kid. Had George Lucas been to outer space? Because there was an uncanny resemblance.

She appreciated the fact Thyos didn't expect her to ride bitch. She got her own bike, and once she figured out the controls, she had a blast zooming through the trees, doing hover wheelies and zigzags. It helped that the vehicle wouldn't let her crash. Some kind of safety feature ensuring she never got too close to any trunks or branches.

She couldn't have said how far they travelled, only that it was fun. When they finally stopped, she was smiling. And dear Lord, he smiled back.

Once more she couldn't help but notice how handsome he was. He'd worn only a harness over his chest and a short kilt for the ride, meaning he had plenty of his body on display. She'd seen even more of it when he'd barged into her room, ready to be her hero.

Kind of hot, especially given he'd been dressed in a pair of loose shorts and nothing else. She got to see those shorts again once they'd parked and he stripped down to dive into a lake, the water sparkling in the sun.

When he emerged from the water, hair slicked back, he showed white teeth as he said, "Aren't you coming in?"

The water tempted, but she could already see it was deep. It went from rocky lip to bottomless.

"No thanks."

"Why not?"

"I can't swim." She hated to admit it and waited for the mockery.

Instead, he said, "Let me show you how."

Her first impulse was to say no. After all, she'd refused more than a few offers of teaching by her friends and the Zonians. Pride and even a bit of fear had held her back.

Not today. Call her possessed, or she was just in the mood, she stripped, her cheeks hot under the avidness of his gaze. Did he like what he saw when she removed everything but her undershorts and cropped tight tank top that acted as a bralette? She could only imagine what the glow in his eyes meant.

Not yellow, she realized, but golden and warm. The

fact they were shining should have repulsed her. Instead she felt more of that delicious heat between her legs.

It might have been a while since those teenage hormones had her wet all the time, but she remembered the feeling. The panted, fumbling pleasure in the back seat of Ryan's car. He'd been two years older than her, driving and so hot.

The breathless feeling was back with Thyos. When he hooked one arm on the rock lip and offered the other for her to take, she didn't hesitate. Her hips swayed as she joined him and crouched. This close, she could see the shape of his body under the water, his legs shadowy in the deepness.

"Does anything live in there?" she asked. There was nothing floating atop or projecting through the surface. Not a single weed. It should have been reassuring.

"Nothing that will come near us. It's safe."

She highly doubted that. Being near him was anything but.

Sitting first on her ass, she dipped her toes into the water, submerging both feet, not realizing she held her breath until her lungs strained. She heaved in some air and tried to relax as she focused her feet in the water. Nothing else.

"You planning on coming in today? I'd prefer setting up camp while there is daylight," he teased, but not in a mean fashion.

"I'm coming." Not yet. But possibly soon. He was attractive. She gripped his hand as she slipped into the water, the chill making her gasp. "It's cold." The water dropped in temperature as it got deeper.

"Only cold until you start moving. Make your body work a little, and it will feel fine."

"Work my body how?" She clung to the lip of the rocky ledge. If she let go, she knew she wouldn't immediately sink. Or was she assuming too much? Alien planet, it might have different laws of physics.

She dropped her chin to stare at the water and could see her toes resting on the rock below the surface. Just her feet, then his were beside hers. A good bit bigger than hers. Darker, too. She liked knowing he was near.

"Push your lower body away from the rock and extend your legs."

She knew what he meant. "You want me to flutter kick."

Ryan had been on the swim team, and she'd watched him quite a bit for the cheap thrills and the making out in his car after.

"Not yet, just hold yourself in that position until you feel the buoyancy of the water."

"You can't feel buoyancy."

"Yes, you can but only once you lighten your body by getting in tune with the water," he insisted.

"Floating is not some magical trick. Either you're heavy enough to sink or you've got some fat or fluffy spots that help you stay on top."

"I see why you don't know how to swim," was his grumbled reply.

"Are you calling me difficult?" she sputtered.

"I think you are arguing so that you can avoid trying. Probably too scared."

Maybe she was a little. This was water. She'd had nightmares about it for a long time.

"You *are* scared. Why?"

Despite having kept it a secret for a long time, she found herself telling him. "My dad drowned when I was little. A fishing accident. Water freaks me out. Took me years before I could get in a bath. I know it was a fluke. People swim all the time, it's just..." She glanced down at the water and trembled.

Suddenly, he wasn't just beside her. Touching and yet not, he formed a cage around her body, his legs bracketing hers, his hands gripping the rocky lip beside her own. "I'm not going to let you drown."

She believed him. She couldn't have said why. But she let out a shuddering breath. "You'd better not."

He dipped his head, and his breath tickled the lobe of her ear. "You're my *sykyrah*. I will never let you down."

Probably the hottest thing anyone had ever said to her. She let go of the rock wall and turned, placing her fingers on his shoulders before she could sink like the heaviest rock to the bottom.

He met her gaze instantly. Glowing, his expression intent.

"You shouldn't say that." Just like she shouldn't be touching him. Touching that bronzed skin proved it soft and warm. Hairless, too, his chest smooth, and not because he shaved. Her lower body dangled in the water parallel to his. They even brushed a little bit. He could have easily pinned her to the rock if he'd wanted.

She eyed his mouth, waiting—hoping—for a kiss.

"I will say what I feel for you because it's true."

There was something highly arousing about having a male, a man of this much virility, declaring himself. Finding her attractive.

Wait. Did he find her attractive? He certainly appeared to flirt and tease but never actually touched her. Was that because he kept true to his word? Or was he not all that interested?

Why was the answer suddenly important?

"Do you think I'm pretty?"

"Pretty seems too mundane a term. Exotic, perhaps."

"Hardly exotic with my red hair," she said, scrunching her nose.

"I like the color of it and the spots on your skin." He brushed a thumb over her cheek, and her breath caught.

"You said I was alien to you."

"I also said you were beautiful."

He had. She couldn't hold his gaze and stared at his chin. "This bond thing you're so keen on. What does it do? How does it work? I assume it's some kind of marriage. Does the woman suddenly become your slave?"

He laughed. "Hardly. We judge on merit, not gender."

"Until someone gets pregnant, I'll wager. Then the woman gets stuck at home watching the kids."

He shook his head. "Some do. In some families, the males choose to raise the children. While others hire the services of someone better suited to the task."

"You mean they get a nanny?"

He shrugged. "If you mean a guardian of children while the parents are away or working, then yes."

"How many kids do you want?" she asked suddenly.

"I don't know. Ask my mother and she'll tell you at least a half-dozen. She wishes she could have had more than four."

"You have three sisters?"

"And possibly a bastard brother, but we don't talk about him," he said with a grin.

She blinked at him. "You have to talk about it. That was a total soap opera mention."

"What does a cleansing opera have to do with family scandal?"

It was impossible not to grin at his oddly literal interpretation. "More than you know."

"The talking helps you, doesn't it?" It startled to know he observed her so closely that he noticed she was calmer.

"Logically, I know the chances of me drowning are slim. But..."

"It is like when you burn yourself. You remember the heat and the pain therefore you flinch."

"That's actually a pretty good analogy." Her nose wrinkled.

"The important thing, though, is to train yourself to not let that fear grow."

"I'm in the water, aren't I? I'd say I'm doing good."

"Very well, which is why I'm going to move away, slowly."

Instantly, she went rigid, and her nails dug into him. "I don't know if I'm ready." What must he think to see her terrified of something so basic?

His expression remained patient, not a hint of mockery in it. "You're ready, and I'm right here. If it helps, keep a hold of me as you draw your body into a straight line."

"Is this the part where I'm supposed to tuck my pelvis and clench my cheeks?" She remembered when Katrina tried to show her in the oily stuff the Zonians used for bathing.

"Your cheeks have nothing to do with it." He looked adorable when she confused him.

She glanced down to his chest instead. It didn't help.

He tilted her chin, and his gaze was soft as he said, "You can do this."

"Sure, I can. I just need to hope my ass floats." She glanced at the water, stalling some more, unable to shed the irrational fear. She'd be fine.

"Ready?"

She almost yelled no. "What if I lose my grip on you?"

"I'm here."

Reassuring words. She took a deep breath, another. He waited patiently. Too patiently.

"If you tell anyone what a pussy I am about water, I will kill you," she threatened. She still had one knife strapped to her ankle.

"This will be our secret," he promised, and then he drifted away from her, meaning her arms fully extended.

She dangled practically without support. If he moved any more, she might lose her tenuous grip. She stretched and leaned forward, trying not to let panic fill her. She kept her fingers relaxed on his skin rather than clinging to him like a leech and screeching she was gonna die.

Barely. She was one heartbeat away from full panic. Her body drifted, rising behind her, lying her flat, but not quite level. Her chin dipped into the water. She might have whimpered.

Immediately, he was soothing her. Kind of. Rather than mouth platitudes, he told her what to do. "Close your mouth and hold your breath if you go under."

"I'm not going under," she muttered.

He did, though. His sudden dip meant she lost her grip on his shoulders. Panic, waiting in the wings, immediately rushed in, and she flailed, splashing water into her face, even opening her mouth to scream and feeling liquid rush in.

Then his hands were there on her waist, holding her steady and above the surface, his voice snapping, "Spit that out!"

She obeyed, thankful he knew what to say because anything else and she would have probably cried.

"Take a deep breath. Again," he said.

She breathed, ashamed of herself. Of her fear.

"Why did you panic?"

"You went under."

"I did. And I'm fine."

More than fine, he was slick and wet. He held them aloft, face to face. He leaned in and rubbed his cheek against hers. Odd, yet soothing.

"You don't have to fear," he rumbled,

"Promise you'll hold me."

"Always."

It was then she realized it wasn't his arms around her but his tail!

TWELVE

"PLEASE DON'T SCREAM. I might go deaf." His tone was dry, but she heard the underlying fear. Was she going to reject him for being different?

She held tight to her panic and took in the situation. His hands were skimming the water keeping them afloat while his tail curled around her. It wasn't crushing her to death like an anaconda or slimy as expected. Hell, she'd thought it was his arm. In a sense, it was another limb.

She glanced at the tail, a bit rougher in texture compared to the rest of him. Gentle in the way it held her.

She smiled at him. "Let's try that floating thing again."

"Are you sure?"

She nodded. "I hate being scared."

"I'm right here."

A fact she kept reminding herself of as he moved away, and once more, she stretched to follow him. This time, she didn't panic when he sank, rather she kept her arms and legs moving. Awkwardly, but she treaded water.

She ignored the water covering her chin and lapping at her lip. She wouldn't let panic prevail.

"Very good," Thyos purred. "Now, put your face in the water and blow."

"Can't I blow something else?"

He must have caught the innuendo, because his nostrils flared and his eyes went molten. "Perhaps later you can show me what you mean. Right now, it's time for your second lesson."

With those words, he sank underwater, though not far. She could still see him. He waved and smiled. He made it look easy.

Damn him. She inhaled a breath and stuck her face in the water.

It wasn't horrible, and after a second, she even opened her eyes and saw him staring back at her, mere inches from her face. It startled a yell from her that was more bubbles than anything. Before she should heave in a startled breath, she was projected above the surface.

She sucked in air and yelled. "Jeezus, don't scare me like that!"

He tucked her close, and his expression held amusement as he said, "Do I scare you?"

He did, but not for any reason he'd think.

"You wish I was scared of you," she snorted, trying to make light of the situation.

"That's good. Are you ready to try again?"

"No," she grumbled, even as she let go of the shoulders she'd been gripping again.

This time when she put her face in the water, she knew to expect his. That was only the first of the lessons.

More followed. He taught her what she needed to

know. Taught and nothing else. Another guy might have used this as his chance to put his hands all over her in a way that had nothing to do with swimming. She kind of expected it, yearned for it even.

He was a perfect gentleman.

She could have screamed in frustration.

The only time he ever laid hands on her was in the beginning when she panicked. Even then, his hands acted in a dispassionate manner, never once inappropriately placed. It was respectful and maddening all at once, which was why that evening, as they sat across each other at the fire she built because she didn't want him to think her useless, she blurted out, "Are you attracted to me?"

"What makes you think I'm not?" was his reply as he snapped some dry branches and tossed them onto the fire.

"You had me half naked in the water this afternoon. Any other guy would have at least tried to kiss me. Cop a feel, something."

Thyos sounded amused as he said, "Are you complaining because I didn't?"

"I'm just wondering. Because you keep saying I'm the one"—and yes she did give him air quotes—"but you act like an older brother instead."

"Would it please you to know that my control is being stressed to its limits?"

"You're just saying that."

"I don't need to lie about my desire for you." The words emerged as a low growl. "I've thought about you since the moment we met. You are in my dreams, usually wearing nothing. In my fantasies, there's nothing we haven't done. Not a part of you that I haven't tasted.

"Oh." She fell silent, unsure what to say next, which was a new thing for her.

"You ask why I haven't seduced you? It is because I made you a promise. And I will not break my word."

"So you do want to seduce me?" She might have said it coyly.

"More than you can imagine."

The statement pleased her. "But you won't do a thing unless I ask?"

"When we come together, it will be of your choosing. Even if it kills me," he added in a dark mutter.

Did he know how close she was to saying hell yeah? "Here's the thing, even if I wanted to, I won't, because from the sounds of it, if we have sex, then I'll have married you."

"Not quite. The bonding of *sykyrah* is more than just copulation."

"Does it involve magical words or some kind of blood ritual?"

"No. And if this is your way of asking if sex will change our arrangement, then fear not. At the end of the bargained eight days, even if we indulged in much stupendous coitus, if you choose to leave, I will respect my vow."

"Why should I believe you?" Part of her was tempted by him, but she worried that she'd be making a lifelong mistake. She barely knew him, and while she was growing to like him, they were still literally worlds apart.

"I can give you nothing more than my word as a warrior. May the goddess strike me down if I lie."

He remained alive. Which meant nothing to an atheist like her.

For sleeping that night, she had her own mattress, a thin foam thing that managed to reduce the hardness of the ground. Her blanket was also thin and yet managed at the same time to feel heavy and warm. She slept alone while Thyos took a spot across the fire.

Still bloody well respecting her. Waiting for her to give in to her hormones. Hormones that were screaming, *Why not?*

If sex wouldn't marry them, then why hold back? Who knew when she'd find someone again that made her feel horny and sexy?

She briefly thought about the human settlement he'd shown her. Maybe she'd find someone there, but what if she didn't? What if he was her chance for a bit of fun?

"Thyos."

"Yes, Belle." There he was with that soft version of her name.

"Promise it won't commit me to anything."

He took a long moment before replying. "I would never force you to do anything, Belle. If you stay with me, it has to be your choice, no matter what happens between us."

For some reason she believed him. That and she was done fighting her attraction.

Rather than waste more time, she rose from her mattress and strode over to his. He was sitting, the blanket over his lap, his upper body bare. She knelt, her knees on the mattress.

"Don't think this means anything." She leaned in to kiss him. Her mouth pressed against his, and it was like embracing a statue.

Didn't he want to kiss her? Was he about to reject her?

"Are you seducing me, Belle?" he asked, his words an anguished moan.

"Yeah." She cupped his cheeks, and that was when she unleashed the storm.

He kissed her back, hard, powerful. The forceful slant of his mouth claimed her lips, her breath, her senses.

He dragged her into his lap, and she felt the hardness of him barely concealed by the blanket, a throbbing presence under her bum.

His kiss was everything. Lips, tongue, sucks and nips, slides and sighs. She found herself astride his lap, her thighs on either side of his hips, her hands cupping his cheeks, kissing him back just as passionately.

His fingers dug into her waist under the hem of her shirt, flesh to flesh. It seemed like too much between them. She pulled out of the kiss long enough to strip it.

His eyes were molten gold. "So beautiful," he growled before dipping his head.

She'd stripped and washed her bralette earlier, meaning he latched onto an erect peak. And sucked.

She felt it all the way to her pussy and cried out. Her fingers dug into the silken strands on his head. She held him and mewled and undulated with each of his caresses.

He sucked and nibbled on her nipples. He switched sides and tugged on her erect nubs, giving her jolt after pleasurable jolt. She rocked and ground herself against him.

"If you don't stop," he groaned, "I'm going to make a mess of the damned blanket."

The knowledge only served to make her more wicked. She lifted herself and reached to pull away the blanket.

There was only scant light from the smoldering fire, enough to see he was built like a human male, if thicker and longer.

Would it even fit?

"Don't fear, Belle." His hand found its way past the waist of her pants until he pressed his fingers against her.

She moaned.

"Do you want me to take your pants off?"

"Yesss," she hissed. She had to help him by lying down so she could slide them off her hips.

Before she could straddle him again, he was leaning by her side, and his hand returned to cup her. She uttered a mewling sound and rolled her hips, pushing against it. He dipped a finger, and she whimpered. Another finger and he began to stroke her, and then his lips found her.

She had a mini climax as his mouth began to play, hot breath on her clit, then his tongue, a bit raspy but very wet. She came hard for him, her entire pussy clamping down on his fingers.

He uttered a satisfied grunt when he said, "You are perfection."

And he wasn't done.

He continued to stroke her ebbing orgasm, penetrating her with his fingers while his tongue lightly lapped. She wouldn't have thought it possible, but he soon had her moaning and rocking again. But he didn't let her come on his fingers.

He shifted until he lay under her, and she was astride again. The hard, heated length of him throbbed against her ass.

"You're in control," he reminded, his eyes a golden glow.

She was in control. She could make him cry out like he'd done for her. She lifted and moved back to sit on his thighs. She gripped his jutting length. His hips didn't buck, but he did tremble.

She rubbed a thumb over his tip and felt moisture. She slicked it over the head, and he uttered a strangled noise.

"Do you want me?" she asked.

"Yes."

"And if I stopped right now?"

"I'll probably die."

She laughed. "We can't have that." She leaned down and blew.

His hips finally jerked.

When she licked his tip, he groaned so long and loud she thought he might be dying.

She really thought about getting him off with her mouth. But…he'd started that fire between her legs.

She straddled him, her hand around the thickness of him as she guided him to her pussy. She threw her head back as she slid down his length, gasping as he stretched her, groaning in satisfaction when he sheathed himself fully and rubbed somewhere really, really nice.

She leaned back to get better penetration, and his hands kept her from falling off as she ground herself against him. When a third hand suddenly appeared, or at least a wet finger did, she opened her eyes to see the tail she'd forgotten playing with her clit.

Perhaps that morning, before she got to know him, she might have screamed in disgust, but now, she screamed because she came. Hard.

And he came with her. They were locked together in a

moment of pure bliss that she could have basked in forever.

Eventually, she collapsed atop him, and he held her, her cheek against his chest and the familiar thumping of a heart.

It felt good. And right. Maybe a place she could stay forever?

Was she going to let good sex sway her from her course?

"This doesn't mean anything," she reiterated.

"You keep telling yourself that," was his amused murmur. "We'll see what your answer is in eight days."

She went to sleep worried he was right and woke to something slobbering on her face!

THIRTEEN

THYOS WOKE BEFORE BELLE, which meant the delicious torture of having her splayed over him. He couldn't believe she'd seduced him.

He'd hoped he wasn't misreading the attraction, but after her initial reaction to his tail, he'd worried. Then, like an idiot, he'd reminded her of it while in the throes of passion.

Things could have gone badly at that point. Instead, she'd orgasmed. Hard. He'd never experienced anything so glorious. But despite the glory of it, they weren't *sykyrah*. The bond hadn't snapped into place. However, he had no doubt it would happen. Soon Belle would recognize they were meant for each other.

Or would she?

That worry kept him awake, so he eased out from under her rather than waking her with caresses to reassure himself. He went hunting, only to find tracks that led right back to his camp.

Belle!

Knowing she was a warrior didn't dispel the panic as he raced into the clearing they'd claimed by the lake's shore. A big beast sat while Belle rubbed its ears and made the most ridiculous noises.

"Who-is-da-big-cute-puppy?" she cooed.

"What are you doing?" Thyos muttered cautiously, doing his best to watch the animal and not startle it as he eased closer.

She didn't reply as she continued to scratch the ears of the wolmoth, a shaggy canine that had a tendency of eating people if it couldn't find its regular prey.

"I-want-to-take-you-with-me-yes-I-do." She rubbed her nose against the beast, and he waited for her to get eaten.

To his surprise, the thing licked her then wagged its massive tail, left, right, *boom, boom.*

"Belle, you might want to step away," he said, slowly edging closer, his hand on the hilt of his sword. He didn't dare draw it yet, not with her head so close to those massive jaws.

"Isn't he beautiful?" She turned to smile at him. "He makes me think of this Muppet dog that used to be on a show my mom loved. His name was Ralph." She turned back to the beast and murmured, "I am gonna call you Ralph. Because you're so cute. Wanna come with me to space?"

"You can't take a wolmoth on your ship," he said, unable to hide his incredulity.

"I guess he might be a tad large, and he probably wouldn't like all that metal."

"I'd be more worried about him eating you when he got hungry."

"He won't eat me, will you, Ralph?" She grabbed its cheeks and rubbed her nose again.

This was it. She'd die for sure.

Nope. The beast licked her. Then rolled on its back for her to rub its tummy.

Jealousy had him stomping around, getting their breakfast ready. He was somewhat appeased when she joined him and smiled.

"Yay for food. I find myself very hungry this morning." She grinned, and like a fool, he grinned back.

He also had an appetite but not for food. Any plans he might have had were thwarted by her new pet. Ralph made sure Thyos couldn't get near Belle the rest of that morning. If he got too close, it lifted a lip and snarled.

Cock blocked by the wildlife. Was the goddess playing a joke on him?

As the day went on, he thought himself doomed to that single night with Belle when she suddenly said, "I think I need more swimming lessons. Will you teach me?" She stripped until she stood naked, and then she winked.

He'd never undressed so fast in his life.

Ralph steered clear of the water, meaning when she kissed Thyos, he could kiss her back. His tail provided the cushion against the rock when he slid into her, the water making her tight. She clung to him, her fingers digging into his shoulders, her breath panting in his ear. When she came, she bit his lobe, and he climaxed with her.

And still the bond didn't snap into place. She'd accepted him as coital partner, but nothing else yet.

They came together again at twilight when her pet

went off to hunt. They were snuggled when it returned, rumbling its discontent.

Thyos held her all night and got to feel her hands on him, greedy and demanding, in the morning.

They spent three glorious days of exploration together. Harmonious days. Perfect nights. She showed off her prowess not only as a hunter but a fighter, too, sparring with him, and when he knocked her on her posterior, rather than be angry, she smiled and demanded they go again.

Less impressed was Ralph, who, at one point, getting tired of being left out, pounced Thyos and sat on his chest growling and slobbering. He could have tossed the animal or done it damage, but she laughed. Laughed deeply and richly, which meant Ralph got its own puegla for dinner—raw of course.

They talked, her of her life on Earth and how hard it became when her father died. "My mom tried, she really did, but she had to work two jobs, and I wasn't the easiest kid," Belle admitted. "Sometimes I wonder if she was better off with me gone."

"Doubtful," was his reply.

"What about you?" she asked, which led to him divulging some of his past.

He'd been lucky to have his father for most of his life, losing him only a few seasons ago to some raiders. She'd met his mother and sister, so he told her about the other two. All of them younger than him but acting as if they could boss him around.

He'd never felt more at ease with or intrigued by a person. She had a sharp wit, dry sense of humor, and a laugh that made him want to smile. The more they conversed and spent time together, the less sense it made that the bond hadn't snapped into place. He didn't recall it usually taking this long. Something must be missing, but what?

It became obvious she liked him, and he most certainly liked her. Surely she wasn't still thinking of leaving? Then again, she'd not once said she planned to stay.

Should he ask her? He glanced at her rubbing Ralph behind his ears and held his tongue. Not yet.

Later that day, he realized just how precarious his situation with Belle was.

It happened when her pet monster wandered off and Thyos was prepping a spit for dinner. Belle had gone to the forest to gather some wood. It took her longer than it should have, and he worried when she failed to appear. She could take care of herself, but at the same time, she didn't know these woods like he did.

Concerned, he followed her tracks and came across her facing off against a wolmoth, but not the one she'd befriended. This one acted as expected, snarling and snapping, its giant paws tipped with claws swiping.

"This is not a nice doggy!" she griped as she ducked under a paw and rolled before popping to her feet.

"I tried to tell you."

"Maybe if we tossed it a treat?"

"Like what? We're its treat of choice."

The beast went after her again, and she dodged, only to trip and hit the ground. She rolled but couldn't get to her feet, and the monster coiled to pounce.

Thyos didn't think; he acted. He roared and unleashed his warrior side. His muscles thickened, his skin hardened, and claws shot out of his fingers. He raced for the wolmoth and slammed it with blows. *Thud. Thud.* Their roars filled the air, as did the grunts and heavy breathing of exertion.

The battle proved tough and messy, slippery with blood from the many scratches he scored. Thyos didn't suffer as much injury due to his tougher battle skin.

In the end, he won. The beast died with a screech of rage that rattled into silence.

But in that silence, something screamed.

Repulsion.

Belle's wide eyes said it all. She looked upon his shifted warrior form in all its serpentine glory and recoiled. In that moment, she forgot the man she'd lain with. She saw the alien.

It hurt.

He could have argued once he shifted back. He certainly came up with speeches in his head about the fact he was the same person still. As they returned to camp, him once more as the male she knew, he remained silent.

He shouldn't have to apologize for what he was. Either she accepted him, or she didn't.

To his surprise, she did return to his bed that night, and the sex was good, but something was missing. She'd withdrawn into herself, and he noticed her eyeing him differently, which was why the next morning he had them packing up their camp.

"Where are we going?" she asked.

"Home." Because he had less than three days for her to come to the realization that, despite their differences, they did belong together. He just didn't know how to make her see it and, given he had only a little time left to figure it out, wasn't too proud to admit he needed help. The kind only a meddling family could provide.

Upon arriving, they separated. She went for a hot shower—that she told Ralph, "Will make your fur smell like flowers."—and Thyos to hunt down his mother rather than indulge in the jealousy that the beast got to be wet with her.

He found his mother in the kitchen with the yellow-eyed Zonian, baking pastries of all things.

"You've returned already?" His mother opened the massive oven and released a wave of heat.

"There was an incident."

"Does this incident explain why a wolmoth is currently inside our home?"

"No. That's Ralph. She's decided to have him as a pet."

"One does not decide to take a wolmoth as a pet."

He shrugged. "It likes her."

"It might like her, but who says it won't eat the rest of us?" his mother asked with an arch of her brow.

"I couldn't exactly tell her to leave it behind," he grumbled.

"A pet? A waste of a creature. Either you eat it or you use it," Ishtara declared. "She better not think she's bringing it on the ship. I don't need it pissing on something important."

He eyed Ishtara. "What makes you think she's leaving?"

The Zonian snorted. "If things were going well between you two, then you wouldn't be here yapping with us."

"Things were progressing decently, I thought, until

the incident." He'd have to admit to the problem if he expected help.

"Did you pass gas in her vicinity? The little humans can be delicate about smells." Ishtara clacked her beak.

"No!" The very idea.

His mother had her own theory. "Do you require some instruction on pleasuring her? Perhaps some documentation on human mating rituals?"

For the first time in a long time, he felt heat rising in his cheeks. "I do not need help in that respect. We were fine until she saw me in warrior mode."

"And?" his mother asked, genuinely puzzled.

Ishtara understood though. "She couldn't accept you're different."

"I guess." He shrugged. "She hasn't said anything, but something's changed."

"You don't think she's going to stay?" his mother asked.

He shook his head.

"A good thing the ship is almost ready then," Ishtara crowed, waddling off.

His mother eyed him. "Would you really let her go?"

"I gave her my word." And he would respect it, even if it meant losing everything.

"A warrior fights for what he wants."

Something he'd been told since he'd learned to walk. "I shouldn't have to prove my worth. I am who I am."

Why couldn't that be enough?

FOURTEEN

ENOUGH ALREADY. They'd been back at Thyos's castle less than a day, and Clarabelle was ready to scream. Actually, what she really wanted was to return to that lake and the enjoyable memories she had of it.

Minus the lizard episode.

She was still processing the fact that her lover with the handy tail could shapeshift into Godzilla. A shorter version at least.

She'd just about peed her pants when he dove at that rabid giant dog. It was a blatant reminder of his alien nature. Worse, she wasn't sure how she felt about it. On the one hand, she knew he was still the same man who'd taught her to swim, who made her body sing, who accepted her for who she was.

Why couldn't she do the same? Why did his tail and differences even matter?

Needing to clear her head, she took her dog for a walk, letting it bound ahead of her as she tried to sort her feelings and come to a decision. She had only a few days left. Stay or go? She'd yet to decide. On the one hand, she liked this planet and could see herself living here. She had a dog, her first-ever pet, and a boyfriend who wanted something more.

On the other hand, she'd set out to find a new home for all of her friends. What happened to wanting to find humans to settle down with? To returning to a familiar way of life?

Then again, how familiar would it be? It had been years since she'd lived on Earth. She'd changed. Could she really go back to a world that didn't have cool gadgets? To a life that involved getting a job, working to pay bills, living in polluted cities?

Her musing was interrupted as a hover bike suddenly arrived, sending Ralph into a barking fit.

"Call him off!" Thyos yelled.

"Down, Ralph. There's a good boy," she crooned, rubbing behind his ears as Thyos joined her. Dressed in very little, she noticed. "What's up?"

"I've received word that a berserker Kulin warrior is slaughtering a neighboring tribe in the landing field."

"So you're going to save them?"

He snorted. "And embarrass them? No. But I am curious as to who the Kulin warrior is and why he's come to our world with a human female."

The words rocked her. "Hold on a second. He's got a woman with him?"

"Yes."

Immediately, she wondered if it was one of her adopted sisters. Had something happened back home and they'd come looking for her?

Was it a stranger? A clue?

She had to find out. "What are we waiting for? Let's go!"

He had only the one hover bike. She straddled the seat behind him, which made her dog complain.

"Be a good boy," she advised her pet. "I'll be back soon."

Clarabelle held on as they zoomed off.

"What are you going to do when we get there?" she yelled into his ear, because he'd not brought much in the way of defense.

"Discern the warrior's intentions."

"Murder from what you've told me."

"It's only murder if it's random. Could be he has cause."

"And if he doesn't?"

"Then I'll handle it."

"Alone?" she asked.

"I'm not alone; I have you," he said as if it were the most reasonable answer in the world.

It was, and she warmed to know he saw her as his equal.

When they neared the field, he slowed the hover bike. "Let's come at them from two directions."

She hopped off, and he zoomed away. She palmed her pistol and knife before heading for the edge of the trees.

The moment she saw the field of battle, she really wished he'd brought backup. The clearing where she'd landed with Ishtara was strewn with bodies, a few of them twitching and groaning. Nothing a few turns in the healing tank wouldn't fix. Amazing the things they could do in space.

She stepped past one injured person who was

crawling for the woods, sobbing. No one that she knew, not that she'd met many folks since her arrival, but she'd rather liked the ones she had. Except for the one-eyed barber. He kept eyeing her red hair and offering to shave it whenever she walked by on her way to the bakery— which happened to be three times since her return. They had a thing resembling a donut with gooshy stuff in the middle that was to die for.

A sleek spaceship was parked in the field, and near it a massive purple dude, wielding a giant sword. More interesting was the woman standing wide-eyed by his side.

A familiar woman who exclaimed, "Clarabelle? Is that really you?" It was Betty, her best friend and another orphan from Earth.

Clarabelle couldn't help but grin then waved, only belatedly realizing she'd not sheathed her knife or gun. "In the flesh. But a better question is, what are you doing here with tall, muscled, and purple? And what's with all the dead bodies?" No need to let the big dude know most of them lived. He might be tempted to finish them off.

"I'm here looking for you."

"Really?" Clarabelle couldn't help but be surprised.

"Of course, really," Betty snapped. "You stopped communicating with me, and I got worried."

She'd not kept in touch after her departure mostly because she had nothing to tell. It never occurred to her that someone might come looking. "I was busy." Busy fighting her attraction. Busy making out with Thyos. Busy trying to tell herself she wasn't falling for the guy.

"Too busy to let me know you were alive?"

Guilt filled her. "The Zonian council knew I was."

"Well, *I* didn't."

"Sorry." An inadequate apology, but what else could she say? That she'd failed in her quest? Gotten distracted by bronzed abs?

Apparently sorry wasn't acceptable. The big purple guy held Betty back, his hands intimate. Her friend didn't slap them away.

Hold on a second. When had Betty met the purple dude? And had they hooked up?

"So what have you been doing, other than ignoring your friends?" Betty finally managed to grumble.

Clarabelle almost winced at the rebuke. "Checking things out. Following up on some interesting clues. Looking for some guys for the other orphans to hook up with." Wondering if perhaps she should tell her friends about the Spa'Rtk'un. Maybe send a few pics.

"You're on a quest to find them some boyfriends?"

Clarabelle noticed Betty's use of them, not us. Last she'd seen her friend, she was training on Zonia, bitching like the rest of them about the lack of men to date.

Had something changed?

She eyed the warrior dude even more carefully. He stood behind Betty and didn't interfere, but he appeared vigilant. She had no doubt he'd act if he thought Betty was in danger. Was that why he'd slaughtered all the guys in the field?

For some reason she cast a glance behind her, wondering where Thyos hid. She had a feeling he'd act just as violently if she were threatened. It made her feel warm inside.

It occurred to her Betty was still waiting for an answer about the whole boyfriend thing. "More or less. Since

Earth is off-limits, we're going to need something, or someone, for the gals, or there are going to be a lot of irritable and sexually deprived women on Zonia soon." She was babbling, she knew it, however a tingling sensation on the back of her neck let her know Thyos neared. How would he handle the wholesale slaughter? Should she tell Betty and her boyfriend to flee, or would that just make them a target?

"And did you find some?"

"Yup. But I don't know if they'll work out. Damned barbarians if you ask me." She insulted on purpose knowing he listened.

"What makes you say that?" Betty asked.

"Because we are," was the gravelly response.

Knowing Thyos was nearby and seeing him were two different things. His muscled body dropped from a tree several yards away, and despite having seen his bronze skin before—having licked and touched it—it still drew the eye with its oiled perfection. He'd eschewed armor today and wore only a loincloth, a sling for his blade, and nothing else.

Betty blinked and stared, meaning Clarabelle had a sudden urge to block her view. Apparently, she wasn't the only one bothered by Betty's interest. Her purple guardian, who had remained silent until now, growled, "This one is mine."

How possessive, and yet Betty didn't appear to mind. As the warrior stepped in front of her, she patted his back. "Easy, big guy. No one's going to take me."

Leave it to Thyos to laugh. "Rest easy. I have no need of your female, Kulin. I have one of my own." He'd gotten closer as he spoke, close enough he could slap Clara-belle's butt.

She squeaked and tossed him a dirty look. "How many times do I have to tell you I don't belong to you?" It was better than throwing herself at him and demanding he say it again.

"Are you going to argue with me still?"

"Sex doesn't make us married, buddy. We had this discussion already."

Too late, she realized how it sounded by how wide Betty's eyes grew.

Undaunted, Thyos offered a lazy grin. "And we shall discuss it again."

She hissed for his ears only, "Don't make me kill you."

"Don't renege on our deal," was his soft reply.

"If you want me to stay, I need an excuse for my friend."

"How about the truth? That you are mine." An answer that she might have repudiated, except he chose to grab hold of her and toss her over his brawny shoulder.

It was unexpected and out of character. She hollered, "Put me down, you thug." She then cast an annoyed glance and plea at her friend. "Betty, help me."

Help her fight the insane attraction she had for Thyos. Help her escape before it was too late.

Her friend angled her head around the big purple dude and smirked. "Help you? That wouldn't be the Zonian way. Seems to me, you've accomplished part of your mission. You've found a male to breed."

"But he wants to keep me." Even more astonishing, she wanted to stay.

"You know what Pantariste would say."

In that moment Clarabelle could hear her teacher. *The mightiest and wiliest prevail.*

Or those with patience. She had only a few more days. Mere days left to enjoy the pleasure. Hopefully long enough to sate the strange desire she had for him before she left and completed her quest.

If she could leave. It was that fear that had her saying, "Hey, I thought you came to save me?"

"Yeah, but as you just told me, you don't need any help."

Her purple companion chuckled. "Now where have I heard that before?"

"Did I miss a mighty battle?" Thyos asked, playing nonchalant as he eyed the bloody field while ignoring the fact Clarabelle hung down his back. With a knife.

She could kill him if she wanted.

The Kulin warrior stiffly replied, "Just a misunderstanding. The one in charge of the guard post thought he could touch what was mine. I showed him the error of his ways."

"Nice."

Men. Clarabelle couldn't believe they would bond over being psychotically jealous. Then again, given how she'd felt when Betty eyeballed her man, she understood better now.

Wait, when did he become my man?

"Are we going to have a problem?" Betty's guardian asked.

"I never did like the pompous idiot. He only got the position because of his father." She could almost picture the curl of Thyos's lip by his tone.

"So we are free to leave?"

"I have no fight with you, although that could change if you plan to take the female I've claimed."

"You do not own me," she muttered low enough for only him to hear.

"I have my hands full keeping my own out of trouble," declared the purple dude.

Betty, trouble? She almost laughed.

But what sobered her more quickly was the realization Betty was leaving without attempting to take Clarabelle with her. "What? You mean you came all this way and aren't going to rescue me?"

"Sorry, but this hero is taken," Betty replied, hugging the purple guy around the waist, making it clear she'd staked a claim.

She had no problem with the guy not being human. Was it only Clarabelle being too picky?

"It is time you accepted your fate, freckled one," Thyos declared. "Say goodbye to your friend."

"No. You can't do this," Clarabelle railed. "I refuse to let you abduct me, you giant barbarian. I'm on a mission, dammit. You need to let me go so I can get back to the Zonian world and let them know I didn't find any suitable males for breeding." Forget the bargain. She should leave. Now. With Betty, before it was too late.

Thyos ignored her. "If you would, Kulin warrior and his mate, could you kindly relay a message to the Zonian home world that, despite their tendency to cause havoc and their contrary nature, my city would gladly welcome any human females who are in search of husbands. We find ourselves short of females at the moment due to a pandemic several galactic revolutions ago."

"I shall tell them. Good luck taming your mate."

"I don't need luck," Thyos exclaimed as he strode off toward the jungle. "I need ear coverings lest she render me deaf."

"Excuse me? Did you just tell me to shut up? I am going to carve off your ears then feed them to you. No, I'll roast them and eat them myself," Clarabelle screeched as he took her away from Betty and freedom.

How dare he use his brute strength to carry her off! Why couldn't she hurt him as she'd been trained to do?

Why couldn't she admit she liked him?

They only went far enough to be out of sight before he flipped her into his arms and growled, "Stop your complaining. I didn't harm you."

"What happened to not manhandling me without permission?"

"You wanted to go with your friend."

"But didn't."

"By your words, it sounded as if you contemplated it. You've yet to complete the terms of our bargain."

She couldn't help but sneer. "Ah yes, your blackmail."

"We have an agreement."

"We do, and in a few days I'll be done with my part."

"You are going to leave," he stated.

"Yes." A reply that didn't feel entirely honest given the turmoil inside her.

His expression darkened. "Because you are repulsed by me."

For a moment she opened her mouth to deny it then frowned. "Not repulsed, not exactly. But I have to take into account the fact you're different." She couldn't help but glance at his tail, flicking madly.

"You've been enjoying that difference."

She felt herself blushing. "I didn't say it was bad. But you can't expect me to make a lifetime decision so quickly. I still feel as if I barely know you. A few more days won't change that."

"How long do you need?"

A question with no real answer. If they were soulmates like he claimed, shouldn't she know? Wouldn't she already be certain?

"I don't know."

"You enjoy my company."

She nodded.

"Is it the coitus? Do I not please you?"

Her jaw dropped. "Hell yeah you please me." She then blushed.

"That is good to know because if you are intent on leaving, then we are wasting time talking when we could be having pleasure." He reeled her close, and she glanced up at him.

How could she even think of abandoning him? What if she never found another man who made her feel like he did?

What if she was making a mistake?

What if...

She needed to stop thinking. Let her only feel.

She rose on her tiptoes and kissed him. Or he kissed her. Hard to tell as they came together in a clash of teeth then a hard press of bodies against the nearest tree. His tail took the brunt of the rough tree bark rather than her back as he thrust into her, the loin cloth proving its use once he managed to shove up her wraparound skirt. She hooked her legs around his hips as he held her by the ass, bouncing her on his cock.

She came so hard she forgot to breathe.

Later, back at his lair, she remembered to breathe but lost it all in a scream as he made her come again.

Over and over, he made her body sing. Their lovemaking was fast, furious, and explosive.

She wanted to hate him; instead she desired him. She tried to remind herself of his alien nature but found it intriguing instead.

And they kept having sex. They only had to look at each other and they were finding a place they could tear at each other's clothes. Why would this passion not abate?

Why didn't she tire of the way he filled her, thick and hard and long? Why did it feel so good every time she clung to him, riding him to a crest of pleasure that had her gasping and yelling her pleasure? Would she ever be able to stop giving in to the passion?

Because that was all it was. Lust. Sex. Hormones. Surely she would break this spell he had on her before the eight days was up.

On that final morning, she couldn't say no to the tender caresses. It was hard to remind herself she had to say goodbye.

Why?

Why couldn't she stay? He wanted her to. Ralph would miss her if she left.

What of her mission?

What of it?

Thyos had the coordinates, and there was nothing stopping her from sending them to her friends so that she could remain here and forge a new life. And if it didn't work out...she'd have a place to go.

The decision made her light. She could almost imagine his face when she told him. He would beam and his eyes would glow and then they'd make love.

Yes, love.

Because that was what she felt for him.

Pure, unadulterated love.

The revelation had her wanting to announce it to Thyos, but he'd gone to deal with some village crisis. Who knew when he'd be back?

Given she had a bit of time, she headed to the hangar hosting the ship to talk to Ishtara. To explain she wouldn't be leaving with her.

Her friend didn't take it well. "What do you mean you love the male?" She wrinkled her beak in repugnance.

"I know it's quick, but I feel things for Thyos. I want to stay here and explore those feelings."

"Feelings? Caw! It's called good coitus. You probably have a child planted in your womb making you irrational."

"I'm not pregnant. I don't think." She placed a hand on her belly and wondered.

"You have a mission to complete," Ish reminded.

"A mission that doesn't need me anymore. I'll have him give you the coordinates once I tell him I'm staying."

"Are you sure he wants you to stay?" The sly remark came from Thuniana, another of Thyos's sisters, who came sliding out of Ishtara's room, belting a robe over her muscled physique. Clarabelle didn't even want to try and decipher the logistics of how that worked.

She'd met Thuniana only briefly a few days ago, under Thyos watchful—and glaring—gaze. Long enough to know the woman didn't like her. And she really didn't care.

"I'm his *sykyrah*." The first time she'd said it aloud, but it felt right.

"Are you sure? I don't see the bond." Thuniana eyed her coldly. "Surely with the amount of copulation you've indulged in it should be apparent by now."

Would it, though, given she'd only just realized she was in love? "Says you. How can you even tell?"

Thuniana rolled her shoulders. "There's not any visible sign if that's what you're asking. It just is. And you don't have it."

"He said there's a ritual."

Thuniana laughed. "Did my brother lie? I'm surprised. Makes me wonder if he's telling the truth about you being his *sykyrah*. After all, males will say anything for sex."

Clarabelle wasn't about to believe the word of someone who'd been clear in her dislike for her. "Say what you like. I'm going to get my answers from Thyos."

"And what if you don't like them? Will you grovel and beg him to keep you?" Thuniana taunted.

"Red Tide begs no one," Ish declared, then to Clarabelle, "Snap out of it. You're obviously quim addled."

"What? No." She was horny for him, but she hadn't lost all her wits. "I don't see what the problem is with me talking to Thyos. I don't trust her." She jerked her head in Thuniana's direction.

"Are you calling me a liar?"

"Yes."

No surprise Thuniana hissed and threw herself at Clarabelle. But she was ready for the other woman and managed to duck enough to shove her shoulder into Thuniana's midsection and lift her off her feet before slamming her to the floor.

It would have been an interesting fight if Ishtara hadn't cheated and jabbed her with a syringe.

When Clarabelle next woke, it was days later in her bed on board the ship without Thyos. Abducted by her own friend.

She went stomping to the bridge and yelled, "How dare you?"

Ish didn't look one bit apologetic as she said, "About time you woke up."

"You drugged me!"

"For your own good. You were going to stay with that *male*." Spoken with disdain.

"Hell yeah I was because I love him."

"Do you?" Ishtara leaned back from the console. "If you love him so much, then turn us around. But do it quick. We're about to enter an asteroid field."

"I don't remember an asteroid field on the way into his star system."

"We left in a different direction."

"Trying to muddy the trail so he can't come after me," she accused.

"Foolish little human. He is not coming after you. He is the one who gave us the coordinates once he realized you were leaving."

"You lie. He would have wanted to speak to me first."

"Would he?" Ish asked slyly. "Perhaps his sister was correct and he is relieved by your departure."

"No, he wanted me to stay. You had no right. I want to go back. We're meant to be together."

"Are you sure?" her friend asked. "Or did you simply settle for the first male who made your quim quiver?"

She opened her mouth to reply and then shut it. Ishtara asked a valid question. Had she fallen for Thyos because he truly was her soulmate or because she'd not met anyone else?

She owed it to herself to know for sure, which was why she didn't turn the ship around. She did think about sending a message, only to hesitate each time. For one, he'd not sent any. And two...he wasn't coming after her.

The disappointment dragged down her spirits. How dare he respect her choice?

Maybe he wasn't her mate after all.

FIFTEEN

BELLE HAD LEFT. He couldn't believe she'd done it and without even saying goodbye.

Thyos had been so sure the bond would snap into place. That she'd realize they were meant to be together.

It never happened. And she left. He moped almost as much as her dog, but at least—unlike some furry beasts —he didn't try and eat anyone.

After the incident with their neighbor—who escaped with all his body parts intact, if slobbered on—he made sure Ralph stuck close by and had plenty of raw meat. It seemed to soothe the beast, whereas Thyos turned to physical exertion. which didn't actually help. He missed Belle.

His goddess was less than pleased. She appeared while he was sword training, not even taking the time to possess a mortal body. She appeared in all her youthful glory, her brows drawn together in annoyance. "Why are you not making babies with the orphan?"

He didn't pause in his swinging at the dummy. His

arm throbbed as the impact of sword against immovable object reverberated the length of it. "If you're talking about Clarabelle, she left."

"And you allowed it?"

He paused to lean the tip of his sword on the ground. "It wasn't up to me. I always said it was her choice." Either she wanted him or she didn't.

The didn't part still hurt.

"You stupid, stupid male! Leaving wasn't her choice. She is only gone because of your damned sister and that bird!" The goddess paced in agitation.

He took a moment to mull the statement and slowly said to ensure he understood, "Are you saying she didn't leave of her own volition?"

"Of course, she didn't! The girl is head over heels for you. She was planning to tell you when they knocked her out and tossed her into her cabin on the ship. They kept her asleep until they entered the next star system."

Which Thyos knew took only a few days. It had been more than eight since she left.

He glanced at the sky then his goddess. "If what you say is true, then she's now been awake long enough she could have returned." Clearly she'd chosen not to.

"She's confused."

"Aren't we all?" he grumbled as he whacked some more at the dummy that didn't deserve the abuse.

"She'll be back?" Karma should have tried to sound more confident.

"Doubtful. I gave her exactly what she wanted." The coordinates for a human colony with all kinds of males for her to choose from.

Bang.

Males she could fornicate with.

Slam.

Someone like her to fall in love with.

Clang. Crash. He stared at the severed dummy at his feet.

"So when will you go after her?" was Karma's dry reply to the savagery.

"I'm not."

"What do you mean not? You need to fetch her right now." Karma stamped her foot, and the whole world trembled.

The idea tempted, but he did have some pride. "I'm not abducting her. If she is my *sykyrah*, she'll come back."

The question being, how long would it take?

And what if she never returned?

SIXTEEN

IT WAS TAKING TOO LONG. The repairs on the ship should have been done two weeks ago.

Two.

Weeks.

Two weeks of being unable to leave this nightmare colony.

How had Clarabelle ever thought she could live among whiny humans again? Had she ever been so soft?

Worse, she wondered about Thyos. She'd been unable to send any messages. The communication system just another broken thing in a string of them.

And Ishtara didn't seem bothered one bit. She was having a grand ol' time on New Galilea, swapping stories with the colonists, getting drunk on their wine.

But all Clarabelle wanted to do was try and salvage the future she'd tossed away.

The colony leader, who called himself General Murphy, sauntered to her side, a portly man with a luxurious mustache and a genial expression. "You seem agitated, niece."

General Murphy had a tendency of calling all the girls his nieces. And the boys his nephews.

"I'm anxious to get going, but apparently, the repairs are taking longer than expected."

"I'm surprised you're in such a rush to leave. Wasn't finding a human settlement your dream?"

She cast him a glance. It wasn't the first time the leader of the colony had shown an odd perception for what she might be thinking. "Apparently I didn't know what I wanted."

For so long she'd had a certain fantasy about her perfect life. This colony should have fulfilled it. It was everything she'd dreamed of, with its humanized dwellings featuring chairs and beds, even utensils like she used to have at home. There were humans here, people who looked just like her.

The females had rights. Held power. But this wasn't a warrior place. Most of them were soft, with only the guards going around armed and looking capable of not dying if dropped into the wild.

It wouldn't be the worst thing to live in a place that didn't require she be on guard at all times. She knew a few of her sisters would absolutely adore living inside a compound designed to keep them safe.

Sounded stifling to Clarabelle.

And it lacked something.

"Is it missing a certain warrior?" Once more Murphy spoke right to her as if reading her mind.

"I never got to say goodbye."

"Would you have said goodbye?" Murphy asked.

"No." An answer she'd learned too late.

"What will you do when you return?"

"Keep him confined to a bed until that damned bond snaps into place," she grumbled.

"And if it doesn't?"

"I don't care. I love him." Tail and all.

"Love who?" Murphy asked.

She huffed as she faced the colony leader. "As if you don't know. I love Thyos. I want to be with him."

"Who are you talking to?"

She whirled to see Thyos. Here. In the bronzed flesh.

She gaped. "Thyos?"

"Surprised to see me?"

"Yes."

"You shouldn't be. You left without saying goodbye."

"You said I could leave if I wanted."

"Did you want to leave?" he asked softly.

She shook her head.

"Yet you didn't come back."

She didn't need a mind reader to know he was hurt. "Does it help if I say I was trying to? The moment I got here I knew it was a mistake. I tried to leave the very next day, but they keep screwing up the repairs. Ask Murphy. He'll tell you what a bunch of incompetent morons the mechanics are."

"Who?"

She turned to wave at the colony leader, only to blink. "Where did he go? He was right here."

"Sure, he was." Thyos tucked his hand behind his back.

"I was just talking to him. Chunky fellow, big mustache."

"Calling himself Murphy?" he asked.

She nodded.

Whereas he laughed. "I do believe you've met your first god."

"God? What are you talking about? Murphy is the leader of this colony."

"No, he's not, caw," Ishtara announced, stomping into view. Amazing how quiet she could move when she wanted to sneak.

"What are you talking about? You've met him," Belle insisted.

"I have, but he's not a human leader. He's a god. Demi-god to be exact."

"Because there's a difference." Clarabelle rolled her eyes.

"You really don't know how the gods work, do you?" Thyos said as if she were the crazy one for not believing in that shit.

"I don't know what you're both talking about, but I would think I'd know it if I met a god."

"Do you believe it now?" A woman appeared, suddenly and without warning, in front of Clarabelle. A beautiful woman, wearing an almost see-through grown.

And what was her first impulse?

She slugged her.

SEVENTEEN

BELLE PUNCHED Karma in the face, and for a moment, Thyos was fairly certain they'd all die. Belle especially, which was why he threw himself in front of her.

"Don't you kill my *sykyrah*!" he yelled.

His goddess, recovering from the fine blow, scowled at him. A terrible thing to see given it involved an actual storm cloud forming over her head, tossing out little lightning bolts. "She hit me!"

"Don't blame me. You're the one that appeared out of nowhere!" Clarabelle yelled right back.

"I'm a goddess; it's what we do." Karma appeared mightily peeved.

Which was when a chubby fellow with a mustache appeared. "Goodness, Karma, what happened to your face?"

"She did!" Karma pointed in accusation.

"The human did it?" The man who could only be Murphy, turned, his head pivoting more than halfway to glance at Belle. "Nice shot."

"What is happening?" Belle's expression showed a hint of fear, but courageous determination held her rigid.

"You are in the presence of gods," Murphy offered with a flourished bow.

"Goddess, actually." Karma grimaced, and the bruise disappeared.

Whereas Ishtara snorted. "Demi gods. Let's keep things accurate."

That turned a glare from two gods on the Zonian, who didn't look disturbed one bit.

"We are powerful and deserve respect," Karma snapped.

"Or what? You'll give me bad luck?" Ishtara leaned forward. "Do it. I dare you."

Murphy clapped his hands. "I say, accept the offer. Think of the fun we could have."

"We? What's this we? This is all me," Karma said, swirling her finger at the group.

"And a fine job you've done," Murphy declared. "His family tried to kill her and, when that didn't work, got rid of her. Then the boy took his sweet time coming to fetch her."

"Because I was trying to respect her choice," Thyos exclaimed.

"He's the only one who did," Belle announced with a hard stare at the gods and Ishtara.

"I am your friend. I am supposed to save you from bad choices," the Zonian declared with a ruffle of her wings.

"I tried to bring you together, but you just had to be stubborn," Karma huffed.

"That might be my fault." Murphy raised his hand. "You know how I like to do things."

"I do know," Karma snapped. "You're always screwing up the perfect plan."

None of that made any sense to Thyos, but he did know one thing. These people—gods, demi or whatever —were standing in the way of a proper reconciliation with Belle, and he was getting mighty tired of it. He'd come here for one thing only, to abduct his mate and bring her home.

It should be noted he'd come to this decision only after much rumination. Thyos never planned to interfere with Belle's choice, but finding out she'd been helped along...

That changed things. Had she intended to stay? Could they perhaps still be together? He had to know.

But it appeared he needed some help. He stuck his fingers in his mouth and whistled, loudly, which brought him some silence.

"Now that I have your attention, be advised that you will no longer interfere with our lives." He pointed to himself and Belle.

"You can't tell me what to do," Karma declared.

"Interfering is a specialty of mine," was Murphy's addition.

"You are tempting me to peck out your eyes and eat them like berries." Ishtara smacked her beak.

Gallump. Gallump.

The steady thudding drew several pairs of eyes and even widened them.

Clarabelle smiled. "You brought Ralph!"

"He missed you almost as much as me."

The wolmoth, running so hard the ground trembled, appeared as if he'd barrel right through Belle, only to abruptly stop so she could hug him and exclaim, "Who's the cutest, wutest puppy dog evah?"

Thyos had no idea what she said, but Ralph panted happily until she whispered something in his ear. Then he turned and growled at the gods and the Zonian warrior.

Belle sauntered close. "That should keep them busy for a while."

Maybe. He wasn't taking any chances. He tossed her over a brawny shoulder and headed back for his ship.

Of course, being his Belle, she had to argue about his methods. "Are you seriously going to make a habit of carting me off?"

"I was told by your friend Betty that it is considered very amorous by humans to kidnap one's mate."

"Am I still your mate?" she asked softly.

Did she really have to ask? He flipped her to her feet so he could look her in the eye. "Do you want to be with me?"

She leaned back to look at him, her hands cupping his jaw. "More than anything. I don't care if we're not sykyrah or whatever you want to call it. I love you. I want to be with you. If you'll have me."

"Always," he whispered. How could she ever doubt otherwise? "I am yours, and you are mine."

"Forever," she said before pressing her mouth to his.

The kiss began tamely enough, but it had been too long. Too emotional a journey as he worried that he'd arrived too late. That she would have moved on.

The passion between them proved as explosive as

ever. They came together in a clash of body parts and teeth, their breath hot and panting as they tore at each other's clothes. Her skin smooth and lightly scented, bearing no one's mark. Which might be why he sucked at her collarbone hard enough to leave an imprint of his mouth.

He wasn't alone in being a little possessive. She placed a love bite high on his neck, in plain view.

He'd wear it with pride.

Given the trees were prickly, he turned her around in his arms and pushed down her pants. She only had to bend over a bit for him to slide inside.

The tight heat of her made him groan. He thrust slowly that he might enjoy the suction of her as he slid in and out. His arm wrapped around her waist, and his other hand was on her thigh, giving him the grip and angle he needed. To bring her pleasure up to the next level, he brought in the tip of his tail to rub her button.

The clenching of her sex muscles proved instant. He cried out, and his hips jerked forward, deep, hard, again and again. He closed his eyes as the pleasure rolled over him, a wave of intensity that froze him and left him floating at the same time.

Thyos.

It wasn't really a sound so much as a warm feeling. It wrapped around him, a hug and awareness. A presence that saw him. Knew him. It went two ways.

Belle.

My love.

My mate.

He could have sworn the connection between them purred with satisfaction.

Coming back to himself, he pulled reluctantly from Belle's body but only so he could fold her into his arms. Eventually they pulled out of the hug and their gazes met.

"We just got married, didn't we?" she asked.

He nodded.

"I am not going to learn to cook," was her first pronouncement.

"My stomach is grateful," was his reply.

"I don't know if I want kids."

"Let me know if you change your mind." He'd prefer his own, but he could be an uncle to orphans as well.

"I don't know if I can sit around on a planet all the time. I might want to explore a little."

"Travel can be arranged."

"I don't like your mother."

"I'm sure it's mutual." He smirked.

"Thanks for coming to get me."

"You're welcome."

"And bringing my dog."

"He's not so bad. Just don't feed him sugar."

"Is it bad for his health?"

He grimaced. "My health. The smell."

She laughed.

And he laughed with her.

Their journey back to his planet was uneventful, with the gods having decided to leave them alone. Ishtara sullenly sent them a message indicating she'd been called home. The only sore spot was Ralph somehow kept finding sugary treats and then slept with them, releasing a gas so noxious, more than once they had to flee the room.

Thyos threatened to kill the beast. To which Belle replied with a threat of her own, "Kill my dog and no sex for you."

Ralph lived, but Thyos's sense of smell suffered.

His mother had a celebration ready to launch the moment they got home. It seemed she was prepared to accept his choice. In her own fashion.

She grabbed his wife by the arms and hissed, "I expect lots of babies!"

"Maybe I'll get a kitten instead," was Belle's saucy reply.

Despite the celebration being for them, they fled it early. Hand in hand, they ran through the woods, taking paths he knew all too well.

He brought his mate to the life tree. A much different tree than when he'd left. The boughs once again thick and showing promise in its budding leaves. A few unfurled at their approach, and she gasped.

"How cool."

More of the foliage fluttered and danced as he made love to Belle under its canopy.

Only later, as they lay under the boughs, did she glance up. "What is that?" she asked, pointing to the burgeoning seed.

He held her close. "The future."

EPILOGUE

THE FUTURE WAS BETTER than Clarabelle could have imagined. Thyos proved to be an awesome partner, always asking her input, wanting her by his side. His annoying mother and sisters moved out, meaning Ralph got his own room.

Which he'd need, since he was a she and about to have some puppies. Thyos didn't know yet. It was a surprise she hoped to soften with sex.

Mmm, the sex. They'd screwed everywhere, every which way, and she still couldn't get enough. Good thing she was on birth control, or she'd have surely gotten started on those babies his mom wanted. But she and Thyos had chosen to hold off. To enjoy each other first.

Mmm, enjoy...

She hunted him down and found him, shirt off, in the kitchen, cooking.

It smelled divine. She leaned around him to steal a bite, nipping him on the pectoral, only to have him spin her into his arms and take a kiss.

Next thing she knew, she was sitting on the kitchen island, nibbling her husband's neck, when she found herself distracted by someone passing by the window.

"Um, Thyos, why would Kryx have some purple lady slung over his shoulder?"

Her husband turned to look. "He appears to have abducted her."

She cocked her head. "Are you sure? Because she seems to be smiling."

OF COURSE, she is, because Dorrys has been waiting all her life for this moment. You might remember Dorrys from *Reverse Abduction*. She's about to *Welcome Abduction* as a means to escape her mother. But poor Kryx, he never wanted to settle down. How will he react when he's not given a choice?

And now for another teaser, because red-haired orphan Clarabelle obviously wasn't the same Clarabelle seen in *Reverse Abduction*...so who was that mysterious human? Find out in the upcoming *Forgotten Abduction.*

SHE AWOKE INSIDE A WRECKAGE, her head throbbing, her eyes blinking as she tried to focus. Every inch of her ached, and she wondered why, even as she stared with incomprehension at the disaster around her.

Her lips parted. What had happened?

A crash obviously.

"Who are you? How did you come to be here?" The voice, distinctly male, had her huddling and shivering, which only served to make him frown wider. "Why do you cringe? I haven't harmed you. Yet."

The "yet" had her uttering a small whimper. She'd never been so scared. Never ever had she felt like this, which led to the realization she didn't recall anything before this crash.

Nothing at all.

So when he once more asked, "Who are you?" she tried to find the courage inside to answer.

In her mind, she saw a red-haired woman with a fierce expression and a name. "I'm Clarabelle?"

BUT LITTLE DID Sade realize she wasn't that brave sister. However, she'll fall in love before she realizes the truth. Question is, can a warrior accept a woman who is scared of her own shadow? Find out what happens in *Forgotten Abduction*.

For more Eve Langlais humor and books see EveLanglais.com

LOOKING FOR MORE ALIEN ROMANCE?

HOW ABOUT AFTER THE APOCALYPSE?

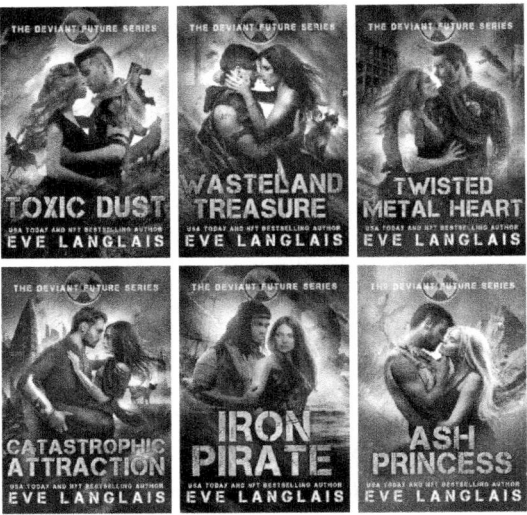

Printed in Dunstable, United Kingdom

70706555R00099